THE
VOLCANO GIRL

To Jennifer
Never give up on
the Superhero within!

ARVIND V. JAGESSAR

Dedication

For Jaime, Rishi, and Ram

GUARDIAN

The night sky was starless and choked with smog. Only the occasional flickering streetlamp gave light to the darkened city street. This was the heart of impoverished inner-city Meridian, where half the buildings laid abandoned and ruined and the roads were pitted and broken. All was filthy, run-down, desolate. It looked almost like a war zone, like a neighbourhood ravaged by armed conflict. And for the most part, it was.

The altered gang members swaggered down the street, not so much walking as loping. These men were mostly in muscle shirts and saggy pants, some barechested, some jacketed. Assorted hand weapons were stuck into waistbands and jacket pockets, including some guns. From her hiding spot in a nearby alley, Neomi could already see the faintly blue-glowing veins under their skin, making a shimmering spiderweb network under the exposed flesh of their faces and arms. Their eyes glowed faintly blue as well; lamplight gleamed on fang-toothed smiles. They were far gone under the mutating influence of the Blue Angel pills; they were barely human at this point.

Neomi's hypersensitive sense of smell registered the oily sickly-sweetness of the Blue Angel taint as the gang drew closer. She could smell the stink of blood and viscera on them too; they had already murdered, and the night was still young. The scent turned her churning stomach. *Not gonna throw up, not gonna throw up, not gonna throw up*, she desperately chanted in her mind, clutching at her belly as the burning bile surged up her throat. Somehow, she managed to swallow it back down, and the nausea slowly subsided to an almost bearable level. *Not yet,* she silently told her rebellious stomach. *Not yet.*

The gang members were playing, some jumping up to perch on the tops of the streetlamp poles, some strolling over electrical lines like tightropes, some leaping into the second and third-floor windows of the crumbling buildings to survey the scene. They were getting close to the residential districts now, where a pleasant night of home invasion, robbery and slaughter would await them. *Not tonight*, Neomi thought to herself, clenching her teeth and steeling her will. *Not tonight. Not in my hood.*

The gang halted as the petite teenager stepped out into the street before them. They regarded her curiously as she moved to the center of the road and faced them directly. Her nausea was so intense now that her belly was glowing brightly, a steady yellow-orange glow shining through the cloth of her frumpy black dress. *Not gonna throw up,* she silently chanted. *Not gonna throw up. Not yet.*

"A young one. How very curious," the lead ganger mused in a deep, surprisingly eloquent voice. The others were smiling, licking their chops, looking very much like predators eyeing some juicy helpless prey. The leader spoke again: "What are you doing all alone in the dark, little girl?"

"You should turn back," answered the chalk-pale young girl, trying to sound bold and stern, but her voice came out shaky and ragged. "This is protected ground, and I am the guardian. You are not welcome here."

The gang members chuckled. The ones up above, on the streetlamps and power lines and in the windows, all jumped down and started to advance. There wasn't really much point in talking to such creatures. Nothing she could say would dissuade them from their terrible hunt, of which she would be their next quarry. But a superhero always gives her enemies a chance.

"Take her," the deep-voiced leader instructed. The gang quickened their pace toward her.

"Don't you know who I am?" Neomi asked, panting, as she felt the bile rising up her throat. "I'm Volcano Girl. And if you dare attack me, you will all perish."

The leader tsk-tsked. "Strip her and hold her down. I'll take the first turn with her."

But some of the gang had halted, looking at each other. A murmur rose from their ranks. Some of them had heard of the Volcano Girl. And even with all their inhuman power, some of them were starting to know fear.

The leader growled with impatience. "Take her! Now!"

That jolted them all into action. They moved quickly toward the girl, long dark arms reaching out for her.

"Now then little girl," mused the deep-voiced one. "I will show you…"

Whatever he would have shown was lost in the seething roar of the flames. Clutching her belly, the small girl hunched forward as fire burst from her mouth, the raging inferno-blast gushing out of her like a mighty geyser of light and fury. The blast was so huge and powerful that almost the entire street before her was immolated for a hundred yards down; lamp posts and hollowed-out vehicles disintegrated and flew away like dust in the wind, and buildings on either side started to crumble and come apart.

Most of the gang members were instantly vaporized, not even given time enough to scream before their ashes and blackened bone-bits were swept away on the burning tide. Some reacted with inhuman reflexes and managed to dive to the side, taking shelter in alleyways and buildings. Two of them bore firearms; they foolishly opened fire at her as Neomi turned her colossal stream of flame toward them, and their leaden bullets disintegrated mid-flight together with their shelter and their bodies under the fury of the flames. The few remaining survivors wisely fled down the alleys into the night, and did not return.

But long after the last of the gang was gone, poor Neomi was left on her knees, convulsively spewing blast after blast down the length of the street, as her terrible power erupted within her fragile body and out through her small mouth. Every few minutes the fiery vomiting stopped, just long enough for her to catch her breath and start to hope that it was finally over, only to start up all over again. It took fourteen agonizing minutes for the fit to finally cease, and the young girl slumped to the sidewalk and curled up into a foetal position to rest. The coolness of the concrete against her arms and cheek soothed her somewhat, as did the quiet stillness, and the sterile ashen smell of a filthy street cleansed by purifying flame.

What a superhero, she thought dryly to herself, as waves of relentless nausea surged and churned in her belly. *What a mighty, fearsome, inspiring hero for justice. She just happens to fall over after she uses her strongest power.   Mighty and fearsome, just not terribly glorious… the comic book heroes never have to put up with this.   Oh boy…   Not gonna throw up. Not again.   Not gonna throw up.   Not gonna throw up.*

* * *

Before

Neomi stood naked before the bathroom mirror, her teeth and her little fists clenched tight, her breath coming fast, her squinting eyes watery and half-closed. She had just stepped out of the shower, so it was time to face the mirror again.

The small young girl in the mirror squinted back at her, her dark wet hair hanging lank and straggly, her pimple-spotted body glowing pale in the fluorescent light from the ceiling. She wasn't fat, this girl in the mirror. She was rather thin, even. But all she could see were the lumps and rolls, along her belly, the sides of her torso, her thick thighs, her hips and her butt. She was repulsive. Self-hatred swelled within her. *Ugly. Fat. Stupid. Stunty. Loser.* The words went round and round in her mind, running through her body, filling her with loathing till she was ready to burst. She wanted to die.

Her stomach turned over, and she doubled over vomiting into the toilet, overwhelmed with revulsion. She never had to put her fingers down her throat anymore, her own self-loathing was all the emetic she needed. Only stomach juices and bile were coming up though; she hadn't eaten anything substantive in two days now. It was the only way she could live with herself, by starving and purging. She was sure that even the slightest bit of food turned to saggy fat on her small frame within hours after eating. This was the only way.

Her father was yelling at her from downstairs. He was angry that she was making so much noise. Neomi tried to throw up as quietly as she could, tried to dampen the violence of it, but it was so very violent. The last thing she needed was to have him come upstairs to slap her. He was always slapping for whatever reason, whether it was Neomi or her mother he was slapping around. She almost preferred that she was the one to get hit rather than her mother, because her mother would turn around and take it out on her. And her mother's sharp tongue left bruises that often felt worse than those left by her father's hand.

But as much of an ordeal that her vomiting was becoming these days, it still felt good afterward. She felt emptied of all that filth now. Empty, clean, light as a feather. But it was time to face the day, and the euphoria quickly faded. She got dressed in a dull fugue. Other girls used makeup, perfume, skin moisturizer and such as part of their dress; she was given neither the items nor the money to purchase them, so she did without. She managed to sneak out the side door without having to interact with her parents; she was grateful for this small blessing. Then she made her way to the curb of the street outside to wait for the school bus, and for the next torturous phase of her miserable day.

The bullying started the moment she stepped onto the bus. *Ugly. Fat. Stupid. Stunty. Loser.* All these words and synonyms thereof flew at her as she made her way to the back of the bus. This walk was the valley of death for the unpopular and the outcast of her school every morning, this walk down the aisle between the bus seats, while the cool kids looked away and the tormenters attacked from both sides. Neomi always got it especially hard because she was such an easy target, and because she had no friends or social clique to seek refuge with.

She sat in the very last row, the "Losers' Lounge," and looked out the open window at the desolate cityscape flying by. Lost in her dreary thoughts, she ignored the other kids and watched the outside as the bus made its dangerous journey through the ruins of the inner-city. Wandering gangs and lone stalkers looked back at her as the bus flew by them. There was little profit in jacking a bus full of schoolkids, but one of these days someone might try it anyway just for fun. The children themselves were cheerfully oblivious; how could they not see the menace outside separated from them only by the thin metal walls of this vehicle?

The bus arrived at her high school, she disembarked after all the others and made her way inside for the homeroom attendance check. She called out "present" when her name was called; she always had to say it several times because her voice was so timid and quiet. Then it was off to class for her, always the first in and the first out, always sitting in the far rear corner of the classroom in her best attempt to avoid attention either from the teacher or the other students. She had a keen mind and could do well academically if she made the effort, but she couldn't bring herself to care.

Lunch time arrived, the best part of her day. She ignored the cafeteria, didn't try to eat or socialize. She went straight to the school library, and from there straight to the comics and graphic novels section. There she entered a world of superheroes and adventure that was a better, more wondrous place to be than anywhere in the real world. She would lose herself in the ventures and escapades of her favourite heroes: the legendary Statesman, Maelstrom the storm-bringer, the mysterious Numina, Manticore the terrible, the shining Luminary, Foreshadow the all-seeing, the invulnerable Citadel, the unstoppable Positron. She loved them all, and thrilled to their adventures and misadventures in the world of Paragon Comics, a world that she wished she lived in.

There were superhumans in the real world, but they were rare, secretive creatures viewed as well-meaning vigilantes at best. And as far as she knew, their adventures were more like the kind you'd read about in Black Dog Comics: dark, and gritty, and grim. Moreover, their superpowers were no fun, usually coming with horrific flaws that made them more a curse than a blessing. No, she'd much rather read about Paragon heroes, and escape to a world where she felt good.

Neomi desperately wished she looked like the women superheroes in particular. They were all thin, and tall, and clear-skinned, and curvy, and ravishingly beautiful. The bullies would have a hard time teasing anybody who looked like that. She would have friends, especially male friends; how the boys would trip over themselves to be near her! And she wouldn't feel so miserably bad about herself, wouldn't hate herself so. Everything would be perfect. Oh, if only.

All too soon, lunch hour was over. The afternoon classes dragged on and on interminably, and she sometimes wondered what was the point of it all. Then, the bus ride home, and the walk through the valley of death in the center aisle between the rows of bus seats. And then, the next phase of her torturous day, her evening with her family, began.

Her mother and father hated each other, and everything in general, and her in particular. She hid in her room upstairs, listlessly doing homework, occasionally switching to re-reading the few comic books she owned, and tried to ignore the sounds of her parents fighting below. She didn't know what was worse, the screaming matches, or the frosty silences; the former drove her to distraction, the latter might presage a visit from one of them. And that meant either a stinging slap from her father, or a blistering tongue-lashing from her mother. Sometimes they would leave her alone all evening…

But not today. It was her father today. Why was she eating his food and taking up room in his home and sucking up his heat and water like a useless lump? Why wasn't she doing her chores and cleaning the house? And then came the slaps, one on the face to shut her up when her eyes started to water, one on the rump to chase her out of the room, hard enough to leave glaring red marks on her delicate pale skin. She actually didn't mind chores about the house, she wasn't especially lazy. But that meant being out of the safety of her room, sharing space with her parents. Nothing she did was good enough, and they made sure that she knew it.

Dinner was usually the worst of it. It was weird that such a messed-up family always ate at the same table once a day; if they all hated each other, wouldn't it make sense to eat in separate rooms or in shifts? It wasn't so bad today, though. Her parents spent most of the time fighting with each other rather than with her. Her father snarled at her for not eating the food he spent good money putting on this table, but he didn't reach across the tiny table to hit her. Her mother harangued her for not eating as well, interpreting her lack of appetite as rejection of her cooking, but she let it go at that. Neomi made it through dinner today relatively unscathed. Then it was off to the bathroom to purge.

She faced the mirror, teeth and fists clenched, breath coming fast, eyes squinting and watery. Even fully clothed, she could see the lumpen misshapen fatty parts of her body. And of course she had no problem seeing her zit-riddled face. *Ugly. Fat. Stupid. Stunty. Loser.* Revulsion churned within her, rose up inside her, exploded out of her. She was on her knees before the toilet, puking her guts out, in an instant. She used to have to wrestle with herself, jamming her fingers down her throat and gagging and struggling to squeeze out as much of her stomach's contents as she could. Now it all came up fast and hard, all by itself.

Her father was already yelling from downstairs to shut the hell up. She struggled to throw up as quietly as she could. It had used to be an ordeal getting herself to vomit, now it was an ordeal getting herself to stop. But she still felt good afterward. She felt empty, clean, light as a feather.

It was back to her room, to try to kill time and shut out the sounds of her parents fighting until it was time for bed. Leaving the house to go to a shop or playground or whatnot was never an option; even if the city wasn't so dangerous, even if there was no chance of encountering the other schoolkids who tormented her, she had no money to shop with and no friends to play with. Better to keep to the safety of her room until she could retreat into slumber.

Sleep was both a refuge and a trial for her. Time passed quickly when she finally fell asleep, bringing her closer to tomorrow's lunch hour ever swifter. But until the moment when her eyes finally closed, she had to face her own thoughts, her own self-hatred, and it wouldn't go away. *Ugly. Fat. Stupid. Stunty. Loser.* It went round and round in her head, and self-loathing churned in her stomach. When the revulsion inevitably overwhelmed her she was forced to get up and run to the bathroom to purge, to empty herself. The vomiting seemed to be getting more frequent and much more violent with every passing day, it was a real struggle not to wake her parents.

After the seventh time, her father was waiting outside the door when she staggered out of the bathroom. Stinging slap to the face, raging admonition to stop sticking her damn fingers down her throat all night. It was pointless to try to explain that she wasn't making herself do it, that it was happening all by itself now. That would just mean more hitting. She squeaked her compliance and fled to her room, her father's ringing shouts following her all the way.

Exhausted, she collapsed into bed. She was empty, but she was in pain, humiliated, wanted to die. The thoughts wouldn't stop spinning through her head, the revulsion wouldn't stop churning in her stomach. *Ugly. Fat. Stupid. Stunty. Loser.* Another night, another ordeal. She couldn't sleep. She needed to throw up.

Neomi wondered gloomily if the rest of her life would be like this. She felt trapped, hopeless. She tried not to think about it. Maybe something would change soon. She prayed so. She couldn't take much more of this.

Eruption

The emergence came without any forewarning or sign of anything preternatural at all.

After dinner, Neomi had been kneeling in front of the grimy toilet of her parents' tatty upstairs bathroom, puking her guts out as usual. Ever since the diagnosis of the stomach cancer, she'd had an ironclad excuse for her purging; it wasn't any damn bulimia. It was the cancer, stupid.

But it was increasingly obvious that this wasn't just an excuse any more, that she didn't have any choice in the matter at all. This cancer-nausea was around the clock, punctuated every hour by the kind of explosive vomiting only seen in the most extreme cases of food poisoning, and having an empty stomach made no difference: there was always stomach juices and bloody bile to spew up. No drug or remedy or therapy had the slightest effect on the relentless nausea; the only reprieve was a flitting moment of relief immediately after she threw up. The night offered no escape; the insistent need to vomit kept forcing her to get up and race to the bathroom throughout the night, and she had no choice but to eke out what little sleep she could in the brief periods between the exhausting attacks. Purging was something she used to do voluntarily, to fulfill a dreadful need. Now she had to purge whether she liked it or not. The irony of being a bulimic who had contracted a vomiting disorder did not escape her.

The cancer had changed every aspect of her life. No matter what else she was doing, she was always struggling to hold off the next round of vomiting and it distracted from her every thought and deed. She was constantly looking for the nearest safe place to throw up and gauging how long it would take her to get there before the next attack came on. Restrooms, waste bins in unused classrooms or custodian's closets, behind trees or hedges outside, between parked cars out on the lot, under stairwells, on the rooftop balconies, any nook or cranny where she could be even marginally out of sight. Carrying sick bags was out of the question as she was throwing up so frequently that her parents refused to buy them in bulk, and furthermore her vomiting was so ear-splitting and horrifically violent that it profoundly shocked anyone who witnessed it. No, finding and using sick-safe spots was the only way that worked.

To cope, Neomi found herself giving silly names to the various types of vomiting she experienced: the "running ralf," the "surprise spew," the "high hurl," the "burly barf," the "yelling yak." She also found herself engaging in "strategic sickness," which was pre-emptively going to somewhere suitable for throwing up and deliberately allowing it to happen, in order to delay and assuage the explosive "power puke" that came on when the nausea inevitably overwhelmed her perpetual struggle to resist it. The power puke was the worst of them all and the most frequent, and the longest she could hold it off was an hour at most; she often power-puked two or even three times an hour, and that was on top of all the other myriad vomiting fits that plagued her. Deliberate purging because she was disgusted with herself was a distant memory now that she was vomiting uncontrollably at least thirty times every day. It was quite a lifestyle change.

Oddly, despite all the misery, amidst the sickness, and fatigue, and sleep deprivation, and dehydration, and starvation pangs, she somehow didn't mind it so much. The endless nausea had given her what she thought of as a superpower, the ability to vomit at will. She was so sick all the time that it felt like she was always at the very brink of convulsive vomiting, so all she had to do was stop fighting it just a little and everything inside would start coming up. She was capable of spewing a fountain of bile and blood up to ten feet away at a moment's notice; it was sadly easy to do considering how often it happened by itself. Not much of a Paragon superhero's power, but it did give her the power to garner sympathy from even the most flinty-hearted people in her bleak life.

All she had to do was cough up a few spouts of bloody bile and her parents, abusive ogres at the best of times, would back off mid-tirade. Even the most vicious bullies had second thoughts when she started to retch, and all she needed to do was retch a bit more forcefully to expel a spectacular fountain to soak them and make them flee. If she wanted to get out of class, all she had to do was spit up a little bile onto her desk and the teachers couldn't get her out of there fast enough. And the dramatic weight loss and clearing of her zit-riddled skin allowed her to stand naked before the mirror without thinking of suicide, for the first time in her young memory. She could handle the torture of incessant vomiting; the torture of self-hatred was far worse. No, incurable stomach cancer wasn't all bad.

So, there she was, puking her guts out after dinner as usual. This particular vomiting fit was the most intense power puke Neomi could remember having, her whole body convulsing as though she was being repeatedly kicked full-force in the belly, the retching coming on so fast and hard that she could barely breathe, the blood and bile spraying from her mouth so violently that the whole toilet and much of the wall behind it was bespattered. And it just wouldn't stop. She was starting to cry from the pain of it, watery eyes clenched shut and hands gripping the rim of the toilet bowl with knuckles turning white, feeling like she was about to turn inside out. It was as though there was something stuck to the pit of her stomach, trying to come up and just urging and urging.

And then, suddenly, the something came up.

She felt the blazing heat erupt in her stomach, surging up and out her mouth so forcefully that her jaws were stretched wide open. Her eyes snapped open, and she saw the fiery conflagration before her disintegrating the toilet and half the bathtub and the entire back wall of the bathroom.

What, one wonders, did she think when she first saw the roiling flames coming out of her mouth, when she felt the burning firestuff jetting up her throat and out over her tongue? Did she feel horror? Disbelief? Amazement? Confusion? Disgust? The explosive blast subsided and was immediately followed by another, and another. Whatever chaos was going on her head, she had no choice in the meantime but to hold her heaving tummy and continue spewing out the colossal fiery jets, again and again, on and on.

Eventually, it did come to an end. Neomi was half-swooning with exhaustion, panting for breath, shuddering. She stared out the huge smouldering hole that had been smashed through the side of the old house, onto a back yard that looked like a massive incendiary bomb had gone off in its midst. It was, if anything, an improvement; the yard had never been tended and had been a patchwork of trash-strewn bare earth and tangles of scruffy weeds. Now the diseased top layer of earth had been scoured away, revealing the purer rocky loam hidden underneath.

Was she dreaming? She wiped her charred lips, and stared at the smear of ash across the back of her hand. Her stomach continued to churn, the relentless sickness quickly overrunning the momentary post-vomiting relief, but it felt like ordinary nausea. She hadn't really puked fire just now, that was a silly idea. Some kind of firebomb had gone off in the backyard and had smashed a hole in the bathroom wall while she was in the middle of a vomit session, that was all. She was probably lucky to be alive and unharmed.

Still… just to be sure, she cautiously opened her mouth and deliberately retched a little, expecting nothing more than a small spout of bile. But instead, burning heat surged up her throat and fire sprayed out from her mouth again, a heavy billowing conical blast easily thirty feet long, shooting from her lips out the hole in the wall and over the smoking back yard. Oh yes. It was real. Her body continued to vent flames out through her mouth for ten long seconds, as if to hammer the point home. It was real all right. When it was over, she got up on wobbly legs and turned to the intact sink behind her, rinsed her mouth and splashed water on her face. Okay then. She felt halfway normal now.

But then she noticed something in the mirror. There was an orange-yellow light shining through the cloth of her t-shirt in the region of her abdomen. She slowly lifted up her shirt to expose her tummy. There it was, right under the belly-button. Her belly... was *glowing*. It was a steady, distinct light from deep inside, as if there was a large burning ember in her stomach, illuminating the veins and internal markings under her skin. She touched her glowing belly, rubbed it with her hand; the skin was very hot, like a strong fever. So... her insides were on fire now? This was outright weird.

Turning back, Neomi looked out through the hole. She still couldn't believe what had just happened. This was serious Alice in Wonderland territory. She bent forward, took a breath, and sprayed fire from her mouth again, sweeping the blazing stream back and forth over the yard until it stopped coming out of her. It was real. She shot fire from her mouth yet again, this time a giant roaring blast that filled the whole yard with flames as it had the first time.

There was no denying it. Neomi could vomit fire. *Powerful* fire, like a weapon far more powerful than any military flamethrower. She was a superhuman now, with a true superpower. She spouted out fire again, submitting to her nausea and puking out the raging flames continuously until she was desperate for breath and ready to faint. And after she caught her breath, she did it again, trying her best to get all the fire out of her body. After a full hour of nonstop flame-spewing, she gave up. Not only could she vomit fire at any given moment, she could continue doing so indefinitely. The inferno inside her seemed inexhaustible, it just wouldn't diminish in the slightest no matter how much flames she puked out. And worse, she couldn't vomit normally any more, it was *always* fire that came up.

Neomi slowly made her way back to her room, and crawled into bed. But even as exhausted as she was, she couldn't sleep. Her stomach wouldn't stop churning; even after all that vomiting, she would need to throw up again soon. And her mind was awhirl. What would she tell her parents when they came back? Would they buy the story of a firebomb going off in the back yard? And how on earth was she going to live her life now? She was a sick girl with stomach cancer, she needed to vomit at least once an hour, often several times an hour. Now that her stomach had effectively turned to an active volcano, how was she going to fit regular explosions of massive destruction into her daily routine? She was now a danger to herself and others, and she didn't know what to do about it.

Nothing would be the same after this.

* * *

Choice

Neomi was a superhuman. She was still trying to get used to that. She had solved the major problems of how to get to school and make it through the day while being forced to expel several incendiary bombs' worth of fiery destruction from her mouth every hour, but she was still dealing with the repercussions and the changes and the sheer strangeness of her new life-situation.

The little benefits were fun at least. Her superior constitution eased the weakness, starvation and exhaustion caused by her constant fiery vomiting, leaving her more robust and clear-minded then she had ever been. She was always toasty-warm from the perpetual furnace in her stomach; she could dance naked in the freezing night rain and experience nothing but a refreshing coolness. (Not that she was prone to dancing naked in the rain. She just gave it a try in a moment of post-vomiting euphoria, and sadly discovered that doing a pirouette immediately made her throw up again.) She was similarly resistant to fire and heat, capable of putting her hand directly into an open flame without any effect, which partially explained why she didn't burn up from her own flames. And her sense of smell had heightened to the point where she could identify individual scents like a bloodhound, even to the point where she could determine a person's emotions through the scent of their skin, although every odor turned her stomach and that wasn't fun.

Adapting her dangerous new superpower to daily life was tricky, but she had managed to pull it off for the first few weeks at least. Getting through the bus ride in the morning wasn't so bad. All she had to do was to deliberately puke her fiery guts out over the empty street before the bus arrived, relieving her nausea as much as possible so she wouldn't puke at full strength during the bus ride.

Dealing with the motion sickness was still a pain though; every bump, turn and motion of the bus made her stomach do somersaults, and she had little choice but to sit in the "loser's lounge" at back and spew out streams of fire out the back window all the way there, making the bus look like it had a rocket engine. The bus driver Maurice was mercifully supportive; he did not believe in discrimination against superhumans, and Neomi's back-blasts discouraged the inner city motorcycle gangs from coming anywhere close, making the bus safer and Maurice happy. What's more, the bullies on the bus were rendered sullen and intimidated at the sight of her shooting massive torrents of flame from her mouth all the way to school, yet another nice little benefit of her new situation.

Coping at school was a different story. She quickly learned that the open parking lot and the back balcony of the school's roof were the only places where she could freely vomit without devastating her surroundings, and had to adjust her tactics accordingly. She already had an informal agreement with her teachers, ever since the cancer happened: she always sat closest to the rear door of the classroom, and when it was time for the next vomit session she could just get up and go without having to ask permission every time. So vomiting fire during class time was taken care of; she just had to make sure she left with enough time to make it to the roof or car lot before the puking started.

Thus far she had avoided any serious accidents, and every day she prayed her luck would hold till the end of the day and the bus ride back. It was pretty surreal that no one seemed to make anything of it, even though her fiery vomiting was regularly seen by other students; it seemed like nobody wanted to believe the impossibility of a girl who could literally shoot burning flames from her mouth, and she was relegated to something of an urban legend. That was just fine by her.

So, on to another day. The bell signaling the end of afternoon class had rung, and Neomi was trudging along to her evening class when she heard the unmistakable sound of some poor boy being roughed up by one of the school's bully cliques. It was coming from one of the lesser used "locker halls," redundant passageways used solely for extra student lockers, generally darkened foreboding areas where unsavoury types liked to congregate. No vulnerable student in their right mind used the locker halls, but sometimes somebody would get caught in one for whatever reason, perhaps from being dragged there, and this sort of thing would ensue.

She paused at the divergence of the locker hall away from the main hallway. She could smell their bodies from here, at least half a dozen of them, stinking of sweat and aggression. This was really none of her business. She should move on. But… she hated bullies. She felt for anybody who got bullied, she knew from experience what a daily torture it could be for the poor soul the bullies chose as habitual prey.
The thought had been turning over in her head for some time now: she had a real superhero's power now. Was she going to be a superhero? This was just like the new hero's trial in the comics. When a new hero discovered their powers, there inevitably came a time when they had to choose whether to use them for good or not. Choosing not to use them for good never ended well.

But this was real life. Real life superheroes usually didn't come to good ends anyway. Furthermore, her only superpower was very dangerous and hard to control, she could very easily cause a lot of damage or even kill somebody. And she was only fifteen! Who ever heard of a fifteen year-old superheroine?

Having a minor as a superhero character was against the comic book rules as far as she knew. What should she do?

All of this went through her head in a flash. That boy was getting hounded and beat up right now. She didn't have time to ponder the implications. She had to choose to do something - or nothing - right now.

Neomi took a deep breath, and turned right. Into the dark locker hall she went.

It was a small gang of seven, but they were piling onto a single freshman student, a scrawny boy about the same age as herself. He was up against the wall, the biggest of the bullies pinning him with his beefy arms, while the others clustered around and jeered. Neomi didn't pay attention to whatever they were saying; it was menacing bully talk, and it was all the same.

"Hey!" she called out to them in her soft quiet voice as she drew closer, some twenty feet away. Whether they heard her or were just ignoring her, there was no response.

"Hey!" she tried again, a little more loudly, to no avail. Getting frustrated, she took a deep breath.

"He-*uuhh*!!" Oops. She spoke too loudly for her stomach to handle, and burning bile surged up her throat as she doubled over spewing flames from her mouth. She retched uncontrollably for ten long seconds, spraying bright billowing gushes of flame over the floor in front of her, then she regained control of herself and slowly straightened up. As the clouds of fire dissipated, the petite, delicate, dark-clad young girl appeared before all the boys as if she had materialized from the flame. All eyes were on her now.

She was abruptly very anxious and self-conscious, and the glow in her belly flared as her stomach swelled with the emotional pressure. How would Valkyrie or Luminary handle this? She had just made a very dramatic entrance… she should continue the drama, no?

Placing her fists on her hips, standing with feet spread apart and chest outthrust, Neomi raised her head high and spoke as boldly and loudly as she could.

"I… I am a hero for justice! And you are villains preying on the innocent! Let that young man go, or I will burn you all with my wrath!"

"What the f@#k is this?" said the dumbfounded ringleader, the tall burly one.
"It's the f#&@#%g pyro from tenth grade," one of

the bullies answered, obviously recognizing her. "She's the one who used to puke all the time. Now she thinks she's a bloody dragon or something."

"Piss off, you little bitch," said the ringleader, releasing the hapless freshman and turning to face her. "Nobody's falling for your tricks. Get lost before I come over there and slap the s@$t out of you."

"My name isn't 'little bitch'," said Neomi, her voice wavering slightly as she struggled with her fear and nausea. "I… I am the Fire Girl! I am a superhero of the city. And I am your bane."

Before she finished speaking the ringleader was already striding toward her, several of his compatriots in tow, cursing at her.

"Go ahead and breathe your f@#$%&g flame at us again bitch," he snarled. "I'm gonna walk right through it, rip your f@#$%&g panties off and stuff them down your flaming mouth. Go on, do it!"

"I warned you," said Neomi softly. Taking a deep breath, she opened her mouth and deliberately retched, stopped fighting her everpresent nausea just a little. Her stomach instantly spouted a heavy stream of fire up her throat and out through her mouth into the open hallway space in front of her, and she struggled to hold it back and keep it from going out of control. The fiery cone had shot out half the distance toward the boys, and she gradually relaxed her throat and let out more and more so that the roiling inferno slowly grew and advanced down the hall toward them. This was the first time Neomi had tried to use the flames to accomplish anything other than emptying her stomach of them. She had never done this before, deliberately shooting fire from her mouth, except for a few times at the beginning in idle fascination that she was capable of doing so without any sort of limit. She already had to spew out fire from her mouth at least thirty times a day involuntarily; she didn't care to do it even more. She had certainly never done it to accomplish a goal or brandish as a weapon. Yet, there she was. And it was turning out to be surprisingly easy.

"Jesus Christ. The freak really is shooting flames out of her mouth," one of the bullies observed, the first to balk as the inferno drew close. "Jesus Christ, that s@#t is hot!"

The other bullies quickly fell back from the blazing heat of Neomi's flames drawing closer and closer. The ringleader stubbornly pushed on a moment longer, till his hair and clothes were smouldering and smoking from the heat, then he too wordlessly turned tail and ran the opposite way down the hall with the rest of his clique. With effort, Neomi choked the flames back down and stopped the fiery stream, and she hurried down the blackened hallway toward the young boy, who was still standing there with eyes wide as saucers behind his owlish glasses. His scent was heavy with fear, but it was also suffused with awe.

"Are you okay?" she whispered hoarsely, and he nodded, seeming in a daze.

"This isn't over, dragon bitch!" the tall ringleader shouted from the other end of the hallway near the curve. "I won't forget this! When I'm done with you…"

Neomi cut off his tirade by retching out a powerful blast of fire toward him, drowning out his angry words in the roar of the flames and forcing him and his gang to flee around the hallway corner out of sight. They did not return.

"Holy jeez," the boy gasped, staring wide-eyed as the roaring flames slowly stopped coming out of her mouth. "You… you can breathe fire?"

She looked at him and nodded, smiling a little. Turning to face away from him again, she opened her mouth and carefully retched up another spurt of fire to demonstrate, just a quick ten-second ten-foot spout down the hall, the smallest expulsion she could manage. The boy, who was smallish and nerdy-looking with his big glasses and mop of curly brown hair, gawked at her some more. Then he seemed to recover his composure.

"Okay... okay. Look. Thanks, but I don't need your help, Fire Girl. I can take care of myself," he said, his voice turning sullen.

Neomi stared at him, hurt. Then she said softly: "My name isn't really Fire Girl. I just made that up. My name is Neomi."

"I thought so," said the boy. "'Fire Girl' is kind of lame, anyway. You should go with 'Dragon Girl,' or maybe 'Volcano Girl'. That sounds more like a superhero name. I'm Darryl by the way. Thanks again Neomi, but I have to get to class now."
She waved shyly at him as the boy walked off at a brisk pace. *'Volcano Girl,'* she thought to herself. *'Volcano Girl.'* She liked that. 'Dragon Girl' didn't really suit her, she didn't feel like an arrogant great dragon with super strength, and wings, and scales, and claws, and fangs. Neomi felt like there was truly a volcano inside her, an almighty active volcano that was constantly erupting out through her mouth, a veritable force of nature she barely had any control over. '*Volcano Girl*,' That's what she wanted her superhero name to be, she decided. That was the name she would choose. She silently thanked Darryl for this little personal revelation. She would remember him.

The next time she saw Darryl was several weeks later. Neomi had secured her reputation as an incendiary character called the Volcano Girl by that point, and many people at school had heard the name by now. She had chased bullies away from their prey several times now, and had undergone her first school suspension and police arrest for destruction of school property. She was also learning how to deliberately vomit in a controlled manner so she could reliably produce blasts of varying sizes and firepower, and a strange sense of boldness and confidence was starting to come over her. Was this what being a superhero felt like? She was pondering that very question when she came upon Darryl again.

She smelled his scent as she was approaching the sound of a scuffle in a locker hall much like the one where she had first encountered him. There was something noticeably different about his scent, a sickening and unpleasant alien odor. There was also the nauseatingly strong scent of many excited, aggressive young male bodies. She had been going to intervene anyway, but when she smelled all this she quickened her pace as much as she could without setting off her volatile stomach.

Within the darkened hallway there was a crowd of young men surrounding a small circular area. It was a fighting ring, as the sounds of pained grunts, physical impacts and noisome cheering made clear.

Astoundingly, though everyone before her towered head and shoulders above her diminutive height, she could see Darryl's head looming over the heights of most of the boys in the surrounding ring. He was *taller*, much more so, than when she had met him. The boy he was fighting was taller still. Both of them were moving around each other in strange, unnaturally fast herky-jerky motions as they exchanged punches. She didn't like the sight or smell of this situation at all.

"All right, break it u-*uuhh*!!" Neomi started to say, but in her anxious excitement she spoke too forcefully for her stomach to tolerate, and the fire gushed out her mouth as she doubled over retching blazing-bright blasts toward the crowd. It was not how she wanted to make an entrance, but this was usually how it happened.

"It's the f*&@*%g Volcano Girl!" somebody shouted, and there were further exclamations and swearing as everyone turned to see the fire-spewing young girl at the entrance to the hallway. The crowd dispersed with gratifying swiftness, all rushing down the hallway away from her as she struggled to stop vomiting before the fireblasts grew powerful enough to reach anyone. When she regained control of herself, there were only two people left in the hall besides herself: Darryl and the hulking boy he'd been fighting.

There was something very wrong with the two of them. Their eyes were noticeably glowing an eerie sky-blue in the darkened hall, and their bodies seemed to be proportioned wrong, their limbs elongated and gangly. The big one slowly bared his teeth at her in a terrifying snarl, revealing gleaming pointed fangs, then he charged at her with that strange unnatural speed.

Neomi was so startled and frightened that fire exploded from her mouth before she could consciously react. Astonishingly, the roiling cone of flames did not stop the boy; he charged right in, arms raised to shield his face, leaning forward into the force of the blast like he was fighting a strong wind. This was the first time that someone had fought back against her power, that the mere presence of her flames was not enough to end any hostility. Close to panic, she opened her mouth wide and allowed the flame to surge up from her stomach and out her mouth in a much more powerful blast, and finally the aggressive boy was thrown back, knocked off his feet and sent tumbling down the hall away from her.

His clothes were set aflame, but the boy didn't even seem affected. He rose to his feet and tore off his burning shirt, revealing a burly body scorched and blackened but only mildly so. Darryl was advancing on him now, and the boy backed off slowly, still snarling with that horrible fang-toothed grin. He kept walking backward till he was around the far hallway corner and out of sight, and only then did Neomi close her mouth and swallow the flow of fire down, ending the blasting stream. Darryl halted and stayed where he was, his back turned to her.

"Darryl?" Neomi squeaked, timidly walking up to him. "What... what happened to you?"

Up close, the changes to Darryl's body were obvious and disturbing. He was almost a foot taller than when she'd first seen him, arms and legs elongated and rippling with wiry muscle. And there were glowing *veins* in his exposed arms, neck and face, making a faintly glimmering spiderweb network under his skin. He looked back at her and grinned slightly; was that a hint of pointed teeth in his smile?

"Volcano Girl," he said. His voice was different too, deeper, distorted, reverberating eerily. "I told you I could take care of myself. I'm a superhero now, just like you."

"Oh!" said Neomi, scarcely believing it. "You're a superhuman too? What... what are your powers?"

"I have a lot," he said, smiling more broadly. He turned to face her. "I'm like a werewolf. I'm strong and fast, I can see in the dark, and I heal quick. And man, it feels good!"

"That's great," said Neomi, yet she was still disquieted and confused. "But that boy you were fighting, he was just like you. How…?"

"There's a way for ordinary humans to become superhumans!" Darryl answered, his voice keen and eager. He reached into his pocket and produced a sort of glowing marble, a brightly shimmering gem-like thing of the same colour as his eyes and veins. It was a beautiful thing, the glow inside it swirling like a liquid. But it had a piercing, nauseating, oily alien scent.

"Here, take it!" he said, offering the gem to her. "They're called Blue Angel pills. I bet if you use them your flames will turn blue and get even stronger!"

But Neomi backed away. The alien thing frightened her, and its smell was so intense that she wasn't sure if she could touch it without throwing up. Darryl shrugged and popped the blue-glowing gem into his mouth. He swallowed, and his eyelids half-closed as the light in his eyes and his veins flared, pulsing brighter in slow, rhythmic intervals. He sighed in deep, intense enjoyment. Neomi backed further away as his body odor subtly changed, clutching her fiery-glowing belly as she struggled not to retch with revulsion.

"Come find me if you change your mind," said Darryl in a deep husky voice. "Maybe we can be a superhero team! How about Angel Wolf for a name? I'll be Angel Wolf and you'll be Angel Fire, and we'll own this place together."

Neomi wordlessly continued to back away. She briefly entertained the idea of pleading with him not to take any more of these Blue Angel pills, but decided against it. It hardly seemed likely that he would give them up now, he was too far gone already. The lure of power had seduced him, and she didn't know what he was going to become. She backed away till he was out of sight around the hallway corner, then she turned and fled, fast as she dared.

She would come to regret that choice. She saw Darryl only once after that. He was with one of the gangs that hunted the inner city, and she saw him through the bus window on the way home from school. He and the gang were barely human any more, not so much walking as loping along on their long twisted limbs, riddled through and through with blue-glowing veins, their eyes blazing blue as if they were tiny windows into a midday sky. She was throwing up through the window at the time, and the stream of flames attracted the gang's attention; Darryl's glowing eyes met hers as his head moved to follow the passage of the bus, and he just stared right through her, a chilling blankness in his gaze. It was hardly likely there were other girls in her school who could vomit fire, yet he just stared at her without recognition, as though he'd never seen her before. That gaze would haunt her till the end of her days.

After that, Neomi vowed never to allow her inaction to happen again. She couldn't live with herself if she did. There was little she could do to stop the students at her school who chose to use the Blue Angel pills, but what she could do was track down the foul scent of the pills and destroy them, whether she had to demand them from their owners or to destroy the stashes stored in lockers or stowed away around the school. She also targeted the drug dealers and their thugs who plagued her school and chased them off wherever she found them, and with them she was not gentle in the application of her flames. And then, she really started to feel like a superhero.

She might be sick as a dog, but she could harness her sickness for good. She was at the mercy of her illness perhaps, but she could also choose to call on it whenever she needed it. That gave her power over her life and power to change the lives of others, and as long as she chose always to change things for the better, she was a true superhero. And that was a choice she could live with.

* * *

Smoke

The blast of swirling flames thundered down the alley, collapsing the plasticrete walls on either side and tearing up the asphalt underfoot, reducing all to smoking ash. When the stream died down, Neomi couldn't see the Angel-tainted gangers who were hunting her in the dark of night, but she could hear faint movement in the near distance, and she could still smell their contaminated skin over the fire-sterilized environs. Unsatisfied, the small girl shot out another monstrous blast of flame from her mouth, passing the gigantic blazing cone back and forth till all the structures and debris in the whole area in front of her were burned away and disintegrated to ash and powder.

In this day and age the city was almost entirely constructed with nonflammable materials, but she found herself wishing for once that it wasn't, so she could leave this area blocked off by a conflagration of burning debris. She had been lured into this maze-like complex of back alleys and small buildings from her home territory, thinking that she was driving this persistent gang of metahumans away from her residential neighbourhood only to find herself lost in the ruins of the inner city, on their home turf.

As the last fireblast dwindled to a wavering stream from her lips Neomi heard movement off to one side, a scrabbling sound of taloned feet finding purchase in the debris. A flash of spinning metal glinted in the starlight. Startled, she turned and violently retched flames at it, and the flying knife was knocked aside by the forceful blast, fracturing and vaporizing as it spun away into the dark. Then she heard movement behind her, a light-footed pattering of someone running toward her. She whirled about to face the new direction and retched out an even more powerful blast, flooding the back passageway. When she stopped spouting the flames to catch her breath, there was no sign of anyone in either direction, but she could detect no scent or sight of charred bodies or bones either. She was in trouble and she knew it. She was being flanked.

Close to panic, the girl cast her eyes about for a means of escape. She couldn't climb or run out of there; such vigorous movements would just make her sick, and she could barely move when she was throwing up. She couldn't simply unleash her most powerful volcanic firestorm to destroy everything around her either, that would leave her exhausted and vulnerable afterward with unknown enemy survivors all around. There was a mostly-intact building not far away, in the direction the knife came from; she decided to take her chances there and plodded over as fast as her roiling stomach would allow. It was some sort of large utility shed, with pipes and gauges covering the wall on one side of it, and a large and sturdy metal door on the other side. There were shuttered windows that she could easily burn through, but they were neck-high to her diminutive stature and her inability to climb ruled them out. She decided on the door.

The door proved to be locked with a heavy padlock. She was halfway grateful, as that meant the thrown knife could not have come from there. She opened her mouth and disgorged a stream of fire onto the padlock, which quickly melted and dropped away. She continued shooting the stream of flame from her mouth as she pushed the door open with her foot; the stream flowed into the building and illuminated a space filled with mysterious rusty equipment and metal crates but empty of anything alive. She hurried inside and reached back to close the door behind her, then turned around and focused her searing stream on the side of the door, melting it into the frame in a hasty welding seal.

Neomi was trapped in here now, but she was also fairly safe. The only ways into the building were the closed door and windows in one wall, which she could cover simultaneously from the back. Spotting an empty wooden crate amidst all the metal ones, she turned her stream of fire on this conveniently flammable source of fuel and set it alight. And now with the pitch blackness of the building illuminated and safe, she swallowed her flame stream and slowly found a seat on one of the metal crates, facing the door and windows, and settled down to wait. Her churning nausea reminded her that she only had half an hour at most before the uncontrollable fire inside her would burst out through her mouth at full strength to ravage this building, but perhaps by then her pursuers would have given up. So, she waited.

She didn't have to wait long. There was skittering movement just outside the door. Even over the smoke of the burning crate, she could smell the nauseating odor of Angel-tainted flesh nearby. She tensed up, readying herself; her excited stomach squeezed burning bile up her throat and she involuntarily spewed out a heavy spout of flame.

But then... there was a solid meaty thunk-sound just outside the door. There was a gurgling yelp, the sound of a body falling to the ground, the sickening smell of tainted blood pouring over the ground. Neomi retched flame again, struggling not to vomit violently. What was going on out there? Were they fighting each other?

More sounds of scuffling occurred, further away and harder to hear. Another body hit the ground, and again there was the sound and smell of tainted blood spattering the asphalt. There was another faint smell that she was picking up now, a dry ashen aroma that was oddly pleasant. About every scent nauseated her to varying degrees, so this new odor surprised and fascinated her. Who or what was that?

The distant scuffling went on for a moment, then there was silence for a time. The scents wafting in from under the door lessened slightly. Neomi wondered if that was to be the end of her night's struggles. Then she heard soft footsteps just outside the door. The ashen scent returned. She startled as there was a polite knock on the metal door. A calm, slightly raspy voice spoke from outside:

"Hello Miss Volcano Girl. I'm not one of these mutants, I'm a friend. I'm going to come inside now so don't be scared."

Before Neomi had time to ponder the meaning of this, she saw a strange cloud of grey mist coalesce in the corner of the building, appearing to swirl up from the ground. From the mist a man casually stepped out, moderately tall and of athletic build, clad in a dark grey martial-arts style combat outfit like a modern ninja, with a black-hilted oriental sword sheathed over his shoulder.

The young girl was so shocked and frightened that fire instantly exploded from her mouth before she could think. The blast thundered through the man and smashed through the wall of the building, leaving a smouldering hole big enough to drive a minivan through. But instead of meeting a sudden fiery death, the man seemed to shimmer into a smoky outline of himself that deftly sidestepped the blazing stream and reformed on the other side of the room.

"Whoa! I'm sorry ma'am," he said, speaking loudly over the roar of the flames, raising his hands in a gesture of surrender. "I didn't mean to scare you. Please don't attack me."

With effort, Neomi choked down the forceful flow of flames and stopped it. She was considerably freaked out, but there was a tranquil air about the strange mist-man that suggested he was indeed not her enemy. Still unable to speak for the moment, she raised her hand in a little wave hello.

"You have trouble controlling it, don't you," said the man: a statement, not a question. "Your fire is limitless and extremely powerful, but it sickens you and it's always a struggle to keep it inside."

She nodded slowly. She saw that the man was of Asian descent, perhaps in his early thirties, short-haired and clean-shaven, handsome in a brooding way. He regarded her with a calm yet intensely focused gaze, and he seated himself on one of the crates.

"We're safe for now. I finished off the other Legionnaires. I'd like to talk, if that's okay."
She stared wide-eyed at him, and slowly nodded

again.

"You've made quite a name for yourself, Miss Volcano Girl. That's pretty remarkable for such a young superhero. Already people are starting to feel safer when they see your flame-light in the night, and the lesser Legionnaires are starting to avoid your neighbourhood and school. Well done."

"Are you a superhero?" Neomi spoke up for the first time.

"Yes ma'am," he said coolly. "I go by Smoke. But my name is Zhen."

"I'm Neomi," the girl introduced herself, and she surprised herself by shyly smiling at him. Where did that come from?

"Hi Neomi. I can see that you've learned to do different stuff with your flames. You can shoot big blasts and little blasts, narrow streams or wide cones. You're fast enough to use your flames defensively against incoming threats. And you can even fine-tune it enough to do utility work like welding. That's really impressive."

"Thank you," she replied, blushing.

"But I think you can be even better," Smoke went on. "I think you can learn new uses for your flames and make your old powers even stronger. I think you can improve your accuracy and your focus, and increase your control so you can stop the flames when you need to. I even think you can learn to manage your sickness so you don't have to throw up so often. I think you can do all this and more, because you have so much power and potential."

"You want to train me, don't you!" said Neomi excitedly: a statement, not a question. "You want to be my superhero mentor just like in the comics!"

Smoke nodded gravely. "Veteran superhumans have a duty to nurture our new brothers and sisters. I want to help you, Neomi. I can train your power and your knowledge and your core of superhuman ethics. But only if you want it. That is my proposal to…"

"Yes!" Neomi cried out, interrupting him. "I want it! I want to-*uuhh*!!"

In her excitement, the girl spoke too loudly for her volatile stomach to handle, and she doubled over gushing a fountain of flames from her mouth. How embarrassing! Smoke came up beside her and kindly rubbed her back while she was vomiting, and when she was finished she sighed and leaned against him. She was so tired, and so sick. But this man's ashen scent was so intoxicating that she felt better just being near him.

"When can we start?" she asked hoarsely.

"Tomorrow, if you're ready. I can meet you at your school after class. And I can take you back to your neighbourhood now if you want."

"I'd like that," Neomi softly answered.

"Very good, Miss Volcano Girl."

The man seemed to dissolve all around her as his cool ashen mist surrounded her. When the clouds began to dissipate she saw the glowing streetlamps of the main street of her residential district; her home was but ten minutes' walk away. When he had offered to take her home, he hadn't meant walking her home; he *teleported* her there directly. Now that was impressive.

"Rest well," said Smoke's faint, eerily disembodied voice. "You'll need all your strength tomorrow. Good night, Miss Volcano Girl."

Neomi allowed her stomach to fully erupt out through her mouth almost as an afterthought, flooding the empty street before her with a colossal inferno-torrent of flame, and then she walked home in a daze, scarcely able to believe what had happened. After her usual bedtime vomit session she collapsed into her bed, exhausted, but still unable to immediately sleep. The delicious ashen smell of the man called Smoke lingered in her nostrils. She remembered how warm and gentle his hands were while he was rubbing her back, and a strange shiver went up her spine. She wondered to herself: she had found a mentor in this rather handsome man, but will she find something... more?

One way or another, she couldn't wait to see what the future held. Tomorrow couldn't get here fast enough.

* * *

After

Neomi stood before the bathroom mirror, eyes wide, hands slowly running over the smooth wet skin of her torso, exploring herself. She had just stepped out of the shower, so it was time to face the mirror again.

The small young girl in the mirror gazed back at her, her dark hair falling in gleaming waves on either side of her elfin face, smooth pale body glowing ephemerally in the fluorescent light from the ceiling. She... she was a rather pretty little thing, wasn't she? Dainty, delicate, slim, shapely. No lumps or rolls of fat anywhere, all smooth and sleek lines. It felt like an alien body to her, the changes were so swift and insidious, but it was a body she could learn to like.

Except for the belly. She ran her hands over her taut, round, swollen belly, protruding as though she was pregnant. This was weird and out of place. This body deserved a flat, toned belly to go along with the rest of her. There was a noticeable orange-yellow glow from inside her belly, as though she had swallowed a burning ember, and that was weirder still. Would she ever get used to this… this body, these changes, the new look and feel of herself?

The light in her belly flared abruptly as her stomach turned over, and she spun to the side just in time as searing flame erupted from her mouth. She doubled over, clutching at her glowing belly as she spewed out the stream of fire through the gaping hole in the bathroom's rear wall, blasting into the already charred and cratered back yard. Ah yes. The other change in her life, everpresent and insistent: her massively destructive fiery vomiting, which she had to do regularly and frequently. If that was the price she had to pay for a body that she could tolerate in the mirror, well… so be it.

All the self-loathing and self-hatred was faint and muted now, in the face of constant relentless nausea. Stomach cancer was no fun. She had exchanged one form of misery for another. But… she knew which she would chose if she had the option to switch back. She had desperately wanted change in her worthless life, and well, she'd finally gotten it. Even if it meant quartering her lifespan, it was still worth it.

Her father was waiting for her when she emerged from the bathroom. He was livid, he wanted to pick a fight like in the old times, and he couldn't reconcile that it was not an option for him anymore. He snarled at her: how was he supposed to deal with this damned hole in his house? How was he to deal with his damned pyromaniac daughter blowing everything up? Neomi just looked at him and shrugged. She had no answers. He started to raise his hand, to punish her for her flippancy. The girl just turned her face to the side and retched just a little, allowing a yard-long gush of flame to escape her mouth. Her father reconsidered, and retreated downstairs. She stared down after him with undeniable satisfaction. There was another change in her life: she wasn't afraid of her parents any more.

Breakfast was a quiet affair. She came down to the dining table and ate with her parents, both of whom studied their food and did not engage with her or each other. She gazed at them and silently asked: *How does it feel? How does it feel to have a superhuman child, eh? A child who could kill you both in an instant? How does it feel?* She would never do that of course. This was just like in the comic books, when a new superhuman was discovering their powers and deciding whether to use them for good or evil. She knew that she would use her powers only for good, as best as she could control them. Neomi would be a superhero, not a supervillain. She might have felt no love for her parents, but she would never harm them.

She managed to choke down a piece of toasted bread and some water. She could barely stand the smell of the toast, but it was better than the horrific smell of the eggs and bacon her parents were having. Afterward she hurried up to the bathroom and waited by the great hole in the wall for the coming eruption. She didn't know how much nourishment her body could derive from the food before it was all burned up in her stomach, but she had to take what she could or she really would starve to death. She gritted her teeth and swallowed repeatedly, holding her churning stomach and struggling to keep the burning bile down as long as she could, but it wasn't long before it forcefully surged up her throat and she fell to her knees vomiting great fiery blasts out the hole. It was always especially violent after she ate anything, as if the meagre morsels of food were stoking the furnace inside her like a shot of nitroglycerine.

Off to school now. Waiting alone at the curb, she allowed herself to resume spewing out flames down the length of the empty street, blackening the road slightly but doing no harm. Hunching over and clutching her glowing belly, she vomited and vomited for fifteen long minutes, doing her best to expunge as much of her nausea as possible before the bus got there. She needed to be as settled as possible for the long ride to school, she didn't want to suffer a full strength power-puke attack while on a crowded schoolbus. The bus was late today and that was a blessing, giving her a few more minutes to recover afterward.

The bus arrived. She boarded and greeted the driver Maurice, then made her way down the 'valley of death' in the center aisle of the bus seats. The rowdy kids went still as she passed by, and the bullies were quite subdued in their taunts. They didn't insult her looks or her weight or her size any more. Now they said "freak" and "mutant" and "pukeface" and "hellspawn". She could hear the fear in their voices though, and she could smell it in their sweat. It turned her stomach, but it was deeply satisfying as well. She was not afraid of them anymore, another welcome change in her new life as a superhuman.

The Goth girl gang near the back of the bus called to her and made a place for her to sit in the 'loser's lounge' next to the rear window, and she gratefully accepted. These were her friends now, and they considered it an honour to count a superhuman among their group. It was surprising how much her habitual dress made her look like them, her perpetually scorched lips the same colour as their black lipstick, her dark dress to camouflage burn marks matching their usual dark clothes. She didn't have piercings or tattoos and wasn't interested in getting any, but that was a minor quibble that no one had issue with.

Elena sat beside her, the first of her superhero fans. Miracles abound, Neomi had fans now! Elena chatted gaily to her about little things, and Neomi eagerly soaked it all up. Sadly, she was unable to reciprocate; every bump, turn and motion of the bus made her stomach do somersaults, and she was unable to open her mouth for fear of spouting flame. Every few minutes she was forced to stick her face out the window, and Elena kindly rubbed her back while she vomited fire out the back of the bus. She didn't care that all the others on the bus could see her shooting fire out of her mouth, for the fact that she was the Volcano Girl was an open secret in her school.

The bus arrived, and it was off to homeroom for her. She would have liked to say "Present!" loudly and proudly when her name is called now, but she was as soft and quiet as always; speaking too loudly was one of the many things that would set off a vomiting fit, including coughing, sneezing, yawning, hiccupping or burping. With attendance taken, it was off to class. Neomi's agreement with her teachers still stood: she sat closest to the rear door of the classroom, and when it was time for the next vomit session she could just get up and go without having to ask permission. This necessity annoyed her now, in addition to the obvious discomfort and fatigue from frequent violent vomiting. She wanted to do well in school now, and having to take two or three puke breaks an hour was making it hard to get everything she needed out of the class. At least she had friends among the Goth girls now, who could help her catch up on missing notes.

Lunch time arrived. She went to the cafeteria first thing, to hang out with her Goth friends. It was very hard for her to handle, with the myriad smells of the crowds and the food all sending her to dizzying heights of nausea, but she gladly suffered it to be with her friends. She even managed to take a little bread and water. Elena accompanied her whenever she had to go up to the roof, and she held Neomi's hair and rubbed her back while she spewed fire over the rail. It wasn't so bad with her or any of the others doing this for her.

Then it was away to the library for comic book time! She had even inspired some of the Goth girls to be comic book nerds with her, and she didn't read alone. It wasn't all fun and games now though. She was a superhero herself now, and she was deadly serious as she read the hero comics with the same dedication she showed her education. For it was indeed educational for her; she took her lessons in ethical conduct, self-sacrifice and heroic intervention very seriously. She likened herself to Infernal, a Paragon character with similarly hard-to-control powers of fire, not her favourite hero but so similar to herself that she considered him a role model. Lunch time came and went with dismaying swiftness.

The afternoon classes passed on without incident, though she chafed for the end of the school day. Today was a training day for her, and she was eager to advance her skills as a superhero. Her impatience expressed itself through her stomach, as most strong emotions did, and she was forced to leave class every ten minutes or so to vomit out all the nervous pressure. When last bell rang, the Goth girl gang converged on her and implored her to spend the evening with them. They were going to shop for music and clothes, then hang out at their clubhouse trying out their purchases till curfew. Neomi sadly turned them down. She did in fact need new clothing, rather urgently so, but a superhero had duties to uphold. Tonight was not the time.

She ignored the school buses and headed out into the inner city ruins. She didn't have to go far; her friend and mentor Smoke was waiting for her. His cloud of mist materialized in the alleyway they agreed on, and the athletic, sword-bearing, grey-clad Asian man stepped out of the mist. Neomi joyfully threw herself into his arms, and he laughed and held her as she cuddled up to him. Smoke was the only one she could freely do this with, certainly the only male, and she took every chance she could get. She found his dry ashen body-odor intoxicating, the only smell that didn't immediately make her feel sick. His aloof bearing returned all too soon, and he stepped away from her. "You won't want to hug me when we're finished today, Miss Volcano Girl," he cautioned her. Neomi begged to disagree, but she said nothing. It was time to go to work.

They materialized in the abandoned shooting range Smoke used as his training ground, and he set about putting her through her paces. First, the warm-up: Neomi was instructed to vomit as hard as she could, but only one fireblast every ten seconds, forcing her to increase her self-control. Inevitably she would start vomiting uncontrollably, but today she got through nine sets of six blasts each and she was getting better at it every day. She would be able to expel her most powerful blasts repeatedly without succumbing to her nausea at all in future. Then, presented with a variety of targets, Neomi was made to spew out varying blasts of flame between her involuntary vomiting fits, honing her accuracy and focus. She vomited narrow streams of flame at solitary targets, then wide cones at multiple targets, then short sharp blasts to repel incoming threats, then she projectile-vomited explosive fireballs to catch distant targets. This was perhaps the most important part of her training, the direct application of her only super ability, and she spent most of the evening vomiting nonstop in this manner.

Then Smoke forced her to practice her athletics: Neomi was repeatedly made to walk or jump as vigorously as possible for as long as she could before the fiery vomiting came on. It wouldn't be anytime soon, but perhaps she would be able to run someday. She was made to hone her breath control, holding her breath as long as she could while vomiting fire continuously, and Smoke marked her record times with his stopwatch. He worked on her pain tolerance as well, putting on the gloves and gently but mercilessly punching her frail body while she struggled to absorb as many blows as she could before the vomiting started. (Her glowing belly remained an obvious weak point however; try as she might, Neomi just couldn't take the slightest impact to her abdomen without immediately vomiting violently.) He then exposed her to an assortment of bottled odors, pushing her tolerance as much as possible before she vomited, and he laid out trails of scents for her to practice tracking like a bloodhound for as long as possible between her vomiting fits. And after all that, the warm-down: Neomi was allowed to vomit freely to let off all the stress and pressure, spewing out the fire any way she liked for however long as needed, just as long as she didn't lose control completely. And then, only then, was she permitted to rest.

Exhausted, panting for breath, smoke spouting from her scorched mouth, her small body dripping with sweat, Neomi looked up at her mentor and said "You're wrong. You lose." He looked at her quizzically, then he startled as she threw herself into his arms again, hugging him close and contentedly snuggling into his embrace. Smoke was not an emotional man, but Neomi was somehow able to coax tenderness and affection out of this hardened superhuman warrior, and she loved every second of it.

Smoke took her home, calling his mist around them both as he held her, and when the mist cleared they were standing in her back yard. He took out his billfold and gave Neomi her superhero's compensation, this time a sum of money that almost made her faint. He couldn't help but laugh, something that he did not do in anyone else's company. "Don't spend it all in one place," he cautioned her. "Remember to budget yourself, save some of it, but get yourself something nice. You deserve it."

After he had vanished into the mist, Neomi spoke aloud what she didn't dare say in his presence. "I don't want your money. I want *you*. I want you to kiss me. I want you to… to make love to me. I want to be your girlfriend. I want you, Smoke." Someday, when she had earned his respect as a superhero, she would say these words to him.

Someday soon, she hoped. She had terminal cancer, and real superheroes like him tended to die in battle. She didn't have a lot of time.

It was still early in the evening; as grueling and lengthy as the training seemed, not that much time had actually passed. She entered the house, headed straight for the upstairs bathroom to shower. Her mother blocked her path.

"Where the hell were you?"

"Training with Smoke," she answered honestly. Why ask? She did this every night, either training with the man or patrolling the city with him. "I learned to projectile-vomit over three hundred feet today, and my fireballs can destroy anything up to the size of a…"

"Is he sleeping with you?" her mother asked bluntly.

"No. But maybe he will soon. I hope so." she answered, just as bluntly. *So what are you going to do about it?*

"You little whore," her mother muttered, but she got out of the way when Neomi glared at her. You just don't talk to a superhero that way, and she knew it.

It was weird and a little precarious showering in half a bathtub next to a gaping hole, but Neomi was used to it by now. No one would be there to see her from the desolate backyard area either, so her modesty wasn't at risk. And with her internal furnace heating up her whole body so effectively, she didn't feel the cold at all. She cleaned up and went to face the mirror.

The small young girl in the mirror gazed back at her, her dark hair falling in gleaming waves on either side of her elfin face, smooth pale body glowing ephemerally in the fluorescent light from the ceiling. She knew this girl was pretty, it was undeniable. If only for that bulging, glowing stomach. She shouldn't obsess about the belly, not when all the rest of her was this sleek and shapely. She had a sexy thin body now. She didn't have to hate herself. She still needed to throw up all the time, but she didn't need to hate herself over it. That was a pretty big change, if she could just embrace it.

Dinner followed, and it was just a chore now, not an ordeal. Her parents were mostly silent. They hadn't figured out how to break her yet, and possibly never would. That was another change she could live with.

After her post-dinner puke, she retired to her room to do her homework and read her comics between the usual vomiting fits, and went to bed early. She was so tired that she fell asleep almost instantly, and slept deeply and contentedly for almost the full hour before her unrelenting nausea inevitably woke her up for the next vomit session. As she knelt before the bathroom's hole and waited for her stomach to turn over, Neomi wondered to herself: would the rest of her life be like this? Training would eventually be over and she would join Smoke on his more dangerous missions, and school would eventually be over and she would move on to city college (or maybe a full time job as a protector of the city), but would life still feel as strange as it did now?

You know, that wouldn't be so bad. It sucked being sick all the time, but life wasn't so bad now. She didn't feel trapped and hopeless anymore. She felt free, and full of hope for better things, for adventure and new experiences and new hardships to overcome. She was venturing into a new world, and nothing would be the same. That wouldn't be so bad at all.

* * *

Forewarning

The thundering blast of white-hot fire crashed against the side of the ruined office building, lighting up the night and ripping through the steel and plasticrete structure like a firehose trained on a sand castle. At its far end, the fiery cone was wide enough to immolate a battleship, easily enveloping the base of the ten-floor building and hollowing it away in seconds.

It was astonishing to see such a colossal force of destruction issuing forth from the petite young girl a distance away down the street, the blazing fire shooting out of her small mouth with such force that the shockwaves were ripping up the street below and beside the stream. Hunched over and clutching her glowing belly, Neomi spewed out the gigantic stream of flame at the base of the building until a rumble ran through the structure; slowly at first, the structure tilted drunkenly as one side of its base disintegrated, then it all came crashing down. The collapsing building fell sideways onto the street with an impact that shook the ground, completely blocking the four-lane road with rubble, sending up great clouds of dust that were promptly blown away by the blasting flames.

"Okay that's good. Try to stop now," said the dark-clad warrior beside her, who was holding up a gloved hand to shield his eyes from the intense light.

Neomi tried to stop, but when this strength of fire was unleashed from her stomach it was very difficult to force it back down. She vomited and vomited for a full minute, swaying precariously on her feet as she grew faint and desperate for breath, and Smoke stepped behind her and held her shoulders to keep her steady. Finally it stopped; she fell to her knees but stayed upright, spurts of thick smoke billowing from her mouth as she panted for breath.

"Feeling better?" Smoke asked gently.

"I-I'm-*uuhh*!!"

The girl tried to answer, but fire shot up her throat and out her mouth as soon as she tried to speak. It wasn't the intense white "Sunflare" fire she had recently developed, but the normal bright yellow-red fire that came out of her when she lost control of her stomach. It was a really huge blast though, rivaling the Sunflare blast in sheer size. She was growing frightened of her own power: these days it seemed like every time she vomited, ever more powerful flames erupted forth.

Her mentor waited until she was settled; Neomi retched several more giant fireblasts down the street, each spout much smaller than the preceding one, then after a final ten-yard blast that was barely big enough to envelop a small car, she slowly stood up. She cautiously rubbed her tummy, which was still glowing very brightly under her sweater, and then she looked up and smiled ruefully at him.

"I got it under control now," she reported. "That's the last building?"

"Second to last," he reminded her. "When the convoy comes down this street you're going to collapse the big building off Rhaegal Road to block their escape. Remember?"

"Oh right. So that's four buildings overall. Do you have any idea how riled up my stomach is right now? I'm so hot inside I can barely brea-*uuhh*!!"

Seemingly listening in on their conversation, her stomach suddenly somersaulted as if to emphasize her point, and she doubled over spewing geysers of fire from her mouth again. Smoke patiently rubbed her back as she threw up blast after gigantic blast down the street, some of the billowing clouds of flame so enormous that they almost rivaled the great Sunflare blaze she had disgorged, but they gradually lessened in size and power until she was finally able to snap her mouth shut and swallow down the flames. She slowly straightened up and sighed, thick white smoke streaming from her mouth, and looked up at him again.

"Holy crap, this is annoying. Like, the more fire I let out, twice as much builds up inside me. Man, I hate my stomach sometimes."

"Don't," said Smoke. "Remember what I told you?"

She winced and nodded. Her stomach and her flames were a part of her, and she was never to speak or think of herself with hatred. That was not the superhero's way.

"You and your stomach are more effective than any weapon or tool I possess," Smoke continued, smiling a little as he offered his praise. "I would have had to use demolition charges to take those buildings down without you. And that would have taken time and munitions that we cannot afford to waste. I know how much you suffer because of your power, but the rewards of using it have been immense. Thank you again, Volcano Girl."

Neomi blushed. She didn't take compliments very well. She wanted to say something flirtatious, but nothing came to mind. Instead, she just shrugged and smiled awkwardly. *Smooth seducing there, girl.* Even if Smoke had any idea of the feelings she had for him, she certainly wasn't making them easy to perceive.

"Let's get to the ambush point," she said instead. "That convoy can't be far away now."

"Very good, Miss Volcano Girl."

The plan was to immobilize the convoy transports and pick off the Legion drivers and escorts with surgical precision, preserving the vehicles as much as possible so they could inspect and plunder their cargo before destroying them. If the convoy was as large and well defended as Smoke's intelligence predicted, they had to be carrying something more interesting than just the usual weapons and drugs. It wasn't her first mission with him, but this was the first time Neomi had been invited to an operation of this scale, and she was determined to prove her worth.

Smoke's human paramilitary allies were standing by as well, prepared to move in to seize the cargo and possibly provide combat assistance if the operation began to go badly. Calling for backup from the humans would be a last resort though; they would be horribly outmatched by the superhuman Legionnaires, and would suffer heavy casualties if they engaged. No, the two superheroes would lead the charge, as superheroes did. It was the only way.

Smoke held out his gloved hand to her. As she took his hand, his cool grey mist rose up all around them, and seconds later the mist receded and they were…

somewhere else.

They materialized in the top floor of a small abandoned apartment building, which they were using as a sort of lookout tower and ambush point. The street they were watching passed below and beside, and the target building was just across the road. When the convoy of Legion transport vehicles passed below, she was to collapse the target building over the road, blocking any route of escape. She had similarly blocked all the roads ahead, so once the convoy was past this point they would be trapped on this small stretch of road, easy prey for her flames and Smoke's weapons.

Even before Smoke's mist had cleared, Neomi smelled something that made her stomach somersault inside her: the oily alien Blue Angel taint, merged with a reeking animal musk like some wild gangrel thing that had never known soap and water. She was terrified.

"Smoke!" she whispered harshly. "Look out! There's something he-*uuhh*!!"

Right at that moment two hellish blazing blue-white eyes appeared at the door frame of the small apartment, and a monstrous growl seemed to rumble up from the floor. Raging fire immediately burst from her mouth before she could think to react, and a huge, dark, furry wolf-body was illuminated within the blazing stream. Her fire was hot enough to instantly reduce a human or Legionnaire body to ash and bone, but this creature somehow resisted it, putting its head down and determinedly pushing forward as if fighting a strong wind.

Behind the beast Neomi could vaguely see through her own flames that another of its kind was charging into the room from behind it, diving fearlessly into the rushing river of fire. Intense nausea and fear ran through her, and of its own accord her stomach forced an even more powerful surge of fire up her throat, stretching her jaws wide open as the thundering blast exploded from her mouth and smashed through the walls and floor and roof around the creatures. The two beasts endured a little while longer, their claws gouging deep rents in the crumbling floor as they were forced backward away from her, then they were torn loose, letting out strangled howls as their disintegrating bodies were thrown tumbling away out of the building to fall to the street far below.

To her side, the blade-wielding Smoke had engaged another of the wolf-beasts that had emerged from a side door, both combatants blurring with speed as they lunged and struck at each other. Had he not been there, the thing likely would have pounced and torn her apart before she noticed it. Neomi turned her head and swept her fire stream through them both. Her mentor's body shimmered into smoke as she knew it would, flitting backward through the stream as the flames swept the wolf-thing up and flung its vaporizing corpse out of the building. That was the end of it; no more beasts appeared to threaten them. Smoke reformed himself beside her as the entire upper corner of the building collapsed before the geyser of fire blasting out of the small girl, the edge of the crumbling floor coming perilously close to her feet as she clutched her belly and desperately struggled to stop vomiting the flames.

The blasting eruption slowly subsided only to be followed by another one, and then another, lighting up the city for miles around as the cycling geysers streamed forth from the side of the building out into the night sky. Neomi's stomach was fearsomely aggravated by the extensive harnessing of its power tonight and was trying to vent out more and more of its inexhaustible fire than she could possibly control, each blazing blast forcing up her throat and out her wide-stretched mouth so violently that her whole body was shaking.

"Volcano Girl," Smoke murmured beside her, gently rubbing her back as she quivered and heaved and spewed the fire forth. "Remember who is the master of your power. You control the flame. It doesn't control you. Easy now."

With every soothing word, the power of the geysers spouting forth from the girl lessened and dimmed.

Each convulsive retch produced a stream smaller and briefer than its predecessor, till she was only bringing up three-second spurts of flame too small to leave the interior of the building. Then she finally managed to choke the fire stream down and stop vomiting completely, and clouds of thick smoke started billowing from her mouth instead as she panted hard and fought for breath. She swayed and fell to her knees, but did not fall over, staying upright with great effort as she gasped and panted.

"All units, hold position and stand by. We had a situation here but we handled it. Watch for enemy attack dogs, and maintain radio silence," Smoke said softly to his throat mic.

Doubtlessly their human allies were freaked out by the light show, flooding the airwaves with requests for information and instructions. Their communications were encrypted, but such heavy radio activity would be noticed.

"What were those things?" asked Neomi in a tremulous voice. "They were so big… and they smelled like Angel taint."

"Legion Hounds," Smoke answered. "That's what happens when you give ordinary dogs the blue pill. It's a bad sign. Only Legion Lords can fully control the Hounds, so that means there might be one of them protecting the convoy."

"And I just put out a signal like a fireworks show to warn them," the young superheroine said bitterly. "I'm sorry Smoke. I guess I'm not…"

"Yes you are," he interrupted her. "These things happen. I know how hard it is for you to control it. You've come such a long way Volcano Girl. Your power has grown exponentially and yet you can control it better than ever. It's inspiring."

"Thank you," she said, blushing again. Smoke shook his head and looked emphatically at her.

"Thank *you*. Neomi, you don't know what you just accomplished. Three Hounds together are a serious problem. There was no way I could take on that many without at least one of them escaping to bring back reinforcements. You destroyed them all in an instant. Sooner or later you'll have to accept that you are more powerful than I am, a lot more powerful. Well done."

Neomi blushed even more deeply.

"So we're going on with the mission? Even though they've been warned?" she asked.

"They will come, or they will not," he said simply. "Even forewarned, we can still bloody their noses if they do come. Keep in mind that we've been tipped off as well. We know there are Hounds and possibly a Legion Lord in that convoy, and we will adjust our tactics accordingly. We shall proceed as planned."

"Okay. Let's do this," she said, a lot more bravely than she felt.

"Very good, Miss Volcano Girl."

They turned to the window facing the road. Here, Smoke had preemptively set up his advanced implements of destruction: a scoped laser rifle, a heavy particle-beam gun, a long-range plasma flamethrower, a variable multi-grenade launcher. All these weapons produced effects that the Volcano Girl had learned to mimic with her fiery oral expulsions, except that her stomach's emissions were considerably more powerful and not limited by ammunition constraints. Together, Smoke and Volcano, they were a destructive threat that few military units could match.

Armed and ready, Smoke took overwatch with his darkness-eyesight and scoped rifle while Neomi concentrated on controlling her nausea, and they settled down to wait. The girl had never taken part in an operation like this before, and she was very anxious. Every ten minutes or so, she would hurry to the elevator shaft in the center of the abandoned building and spend a few minutes vomiting out all the nervous pressure, spewing the fire safely down the empty shaft where it would not be seen from the outside. There was nothing she could do about the noise, but at least it wasn't likely that she would be heard all the way from the street down below.

An hour passed, then another. Had the convoy been delayed, or had they weighed the risks and canceled their own mission? Neomi's vomiting fits became more frequent and violent as she grew more and more nervous, and the glow from her belly was so bright that she was concerned it might be seen from their window and give away their position. She struggled to meditate and calm herself as she had been taught, but she didn't feel much like a superhero at the moment.

Eventually, Smoke said softly: "I hear them," and Neomi herself caught a whiff of vehicle exhaust on the rising wind.

The girl was so excited that she retched a heavy gush of flame out the window before she could stop herself, and her mentor gave her an amused look as she clapped her hands on her mouth and struggled to control herself. He didn't have to chide her that she really shouldn't do that once the convoy came into view.

And then, they came into view. Neomi could not see in the dark as her companion could, but she was able to make out a procession of vehicle headlamps through the darkness and smog. It seemed like there were quite a lot of them.

"Eight vehicles in all," Smoke reported, gazing through his rifle's scope. "Pickup truck with mounted machine gun up front, followed by a troop truck. Then four trailer transports, and then another troop carrier and pickup gun-truck in back. That's twice as many as I was expecting. It's going to be a real blow for them to lose a convoy this big."

"Any Hounds?" she asked, worried.

"Not yet. They would be in the troop carriers if anywhere. Here they come… get ready," her mentor murmured, then spoke into his throat mic: "All units, tangos in sight. Be advised: hostile units at double strength. Prepare for action."

Neomi ducked below the level of the window as the engine sounds of the vehicles rumbled on from below. She readied herself, and her stomach churned horribly as the fiery yellow-orange glow in her belly turned to a piercing white. A long, nerve-wracking minute passed.

"Stand by… they're not past yet… stand by…"

The girl's belly glowed fiercely. Her stomach didn't want to stand by. She swallowed hard. *Not gonna throw up… not yet… not gonna throw up…*

"Now!"

The young girl jumped to her feet, and she threw herself half over the window sill as a titanic blast of blazing white-hot Sunfire erupted from her small mouth. The flames crashed against the base of the opposite apartment building in waves as she threw up blast after blast of pure solar power onto the building across the street. They were far more powerful than the Sunflares she had used to take down the previous buildings, and the target building swayed, tilted, and then came crashing down onto the road within seconds. The ground shook, and clouds of plasticrete dust went up into the night air.

"Light 'em up!" Smoke ordered as they moved into phase two of the assault.

The glow in the Volcano Girl's belly rapidly changed to a hellish deep red glare, and her nausea surged to dizzying levels as her body prepared itself. She finished the last expulsion of Sunfire and sucked in a deep breath, then a great fountain of gooey crimson-glowing fluid gushed out of her mouth, igniting into brilliant red flame on contact with the air as it sprayed outward in a wide cone and came apart like a cloud of falling meteors.

It was an astonishing volume of fluid, a hundred times more than the girl's small body should be able to contain, spouting outward like a volcanic geyser and then coming down all over the road and the convoy below in a deluging rain of crimson fire. Wherever the flaming globs splattered on the ground or the vehicles, great pillars of flame erupted on the spot from the burning magma-like fluid, and the whole area was soon brilliantly illuminated by the conflagration.

When they had discovered this new application of Neomi's power, Smoke had called the gluey stuff "Magmite," a portmanteau of 'magma' and 'thermite,' aptly describing a substance with the consistency of molten lava that burned intensely and persistently like chemical incendiary fuel. It was a frightening weapon, but it was also useful as a source of light in the dark, or as a way to lay down a wall of fire to block off escape or pursuit. In this case, the duo were using her Magmite to accomplish all three of these functions.

Down below, with the street all aflame and night's darkness dispelled, Neomi could see through the stream of her own fiery vomit that the convoy had stopped. Smoke had predicted they would race away only to be stymied by the road blockages, but this outcome wasn't unexpected. The Legionnaires, their eyes glowing like blue-white pinpricks far below, had dismounted and were swarming with activity: taking up defensive positions, extinguishing fires on the vehicles, searching for their attackers.

Some of the altered gangers were raising firearms; a hissing whipcrack rang out as Smoke's sniper rifle burned a small neat hole through the head of the foremost mounted machinegun operator, and then another whipcrack took out a Legionnaire with a long rifle, then another finished off the other mounted gunner in the rear, ringing out again and again as the warrior dispatched each foe that posed a long-range threat.

Neomi's heart was pounding with excitement. This was some real superhero stuff. She was battling her hated foes directly, with her superhero role-model and dear friend at her side. She was proving herself to him, to *herself* even, and sending a grim message to the enemies of this city.

She finished spewing out the Magmite geyser, and the glow in her belly changed back to its normal fiery yellow-orange. Time for phase three. Taking another deep breath, she began retching forcefully at the convoy below, streaking fireballs flying from her mouth with each retch to detonate like grenades amidst the Legionnaires and their vehicles. The Legion fighters were thrown into disarray from the dual assault, their troops scattered and their escort trucks smashed to scrap by the exploding fireballs while anyone with firearms was picked off one by one by Smoke's merciless sniping.

Neomi barely had time to register a strange dark shadow seeping forth from one of the troop trucks before Smoke was suddenly behind her, his arms wrapping around her small body with his gloved hand clamped on her mouth, and she was yanked away from the window. What was happening?

"All units! Abort, abort, abort! The operation is compromised! Fall back all units, *now*!" Smoke was whispering harshly to his throat mic. Neomi was stunned as she recognized the fear in his normally imperturbable voice, as she smelt the acrid musk of fear pervading his ashen body odor. Smoke was... afraid? Impossible! Nothing on Earth could frighten this hardened superhuman warrior, she had been certain of it.

Whatever could scare Smoke really scared her. Her agitated stomach squirted burning bile up her throat, forcing her to retch out a big spout of flame; her mentor's hand blurred into mist for a moment as the fire passed harmlessly through his palm to splash against the debris on the other side of the room, then his hand reformed around her mouth and gripped on tight.

"Stay calm, and don't move," Smoke whispered into her ear. "He can see life force patterns, but we're far away and out of view. We still have a chance."

A long minute passed, both of them sitting on the floor completely motionless. Neomi would have very much enjoyed such close bodily contact with him in other circumstances, but she was sick with fear now. Eventually he relaxed somewhat and took his hand off her mouth.

"I think we're safe for the moment. He would have shadow-walked here by now if he'd seen us," he said softly.

"Who? Who's out there, Smoke?" she squeaked.

"You wanted to know about our opposite number? Take a peek, but be careful. That's what a real supervillain looks like."

Neomi gulped, struggling not to spout flame again. She wasn't sure that she wanted to know anymore, but some fatal need drove her to rise up to her knees and peek around the corner of the window. She knew what she was looking for immediately.

Even at this range, the man's height was quite intimidating. He had on ragged denim clothes under a torn leather long-coat, and a battered fedora on his head, all in black. He was laden with weaponry: the long handles of two very large swords jutted over one shoulder, and two massive long-barreled pistols hung from his belt. She couldn't make out his face under the shadow of his hat, but long straggly black hair flowed out from under his hat brim, and she could see the cold blue gleam of his glowing eyes. A massive slavering Hound stood on either side of him, but the most prominent feature of the man was his shadow.

Darkness flowed all around the tall man like a swirling pool, casting long weird-moving shadows on the side of the nearby troop truck and seeming to draw in all the surrounding light like a whirlpool in black. As Neomi watched on, the menacing stranger drew one of his great longswords and casually prodded a blazing puddle of Magmite. The pillar of crimson flame tilted as if being blown by a strong wind, and was little-by-little sucked into the blade like steam into a vacuum cleaner. Then, as if in a nightmare, the man slowly turned his head in her direction, and his gaze gradually started rising upward toward Neomi's position.

The girl almost yelped with terror as she hurriedly ducked below the level of the window sill again. She looked at Smoke, but her mentor was just gazing off at nothing, almost as if in contemplation. Fear still pervaded his scent.

"Did he see you?" he asked.

"I don't think so. Who... what is that *thing*?" Neomi whispered harshly.

"A great enforcer of the Legion. Finn Moxxa is his human name, but we all know him as Nemesis. Neomi, don't you ever try to take him on, with or without me. He's the one creature in this city that would kill either of us in any battle."

"But... you can't be killed," she said, trembling. "You just turn to smoke if anything hurts you."

Smoke just turned his head to look at her, and she was shocked to see the quiet sadness in his eyes.

"We're all clear?" he said into his throat mic, not answering her. "All right. Go home boys. Thanks for coming out, I'll be in touch with the debrief. Smoke signing off."

"Smoke?" she asked, prompting him. He still didn't reply, he just took her hand as his cool mists rose up all around them, taking them away to somewhere else.

Later, in one of Smoke's safe houses, the superhuman warrior was sitting on a ragged sofa in the armory absentmindedly cleaning a submachinegun when Neomi approached him. With uncharacteristic boldness, the young girl grabbed the weapon away from her mentor's hands and dropped it on the workbench beside them, then she sat down in his lap and pulled his arms around her small body, gently forcing him to embrace her. He didn't push her away, and she snuggled happily into his warm embrace. He obligingly began caressing her body through her dress, his gentle hands stroking and rubbing her back and her thighs and her glowing belly, and thick ribbons of white smoke streamed from her mouth as she sighed repeatedly in deep enjoyment. He still wouldn't put his hand between her legs however, even though she bluntly hiked up her skirt and spread her thighs wide apart whenever his stroking hand passed near her knees, but that would surely happen in time, and she was appeased with this level of intimacy for the time being.

After a long blissful while, she spoke to him. "Zhen, what did you mean out there on the mission? When you said Nemesis could kill us, I mean. How could he kill you? I've seen knives and bullets hit you, and you just turn to smoke and they pass right through you, even if you didn't see them coming. How could that Finn Moxxa hurt you if you can't be…?"

Her voice trailed off. Smoke didn't answer for a long moment, but eventually he replied.

"My body can't be harmed by physical means, that is true. But this body isn't… me. It's just a projection, a sort of echo of who I once was. My sword holds my actual life force. The sword is indestructible to most things as well, but some things can damage it. If the sword was to be destroyed, then I would die permanently. And the blades of Finn Moxxa can break my sword. He knows this. That's why I fear him."

Neomi was silent for a time, processing this new information.

"Your body is a... a projection?" she asked slowly. She took one of his hands and held it up, curiously traced the lines in his palm with her fingers. "Do you mean... you're not real?"

Her mentor smiled. "You have a shadow. That shadow is real. My body is the shadow of a sword. It's as real as your shadow, just that this shadow can hold things, and see things, and speak, and eat, and do just about everything a real human body could do. It's an exact replica of the body and mind of the original Zhen Xiaolong who died in China three hundred years ago. The body and mind of Zhen Xiaolong, and the soul of this black sword. That is who Smoke really is."

Again, Neomi was silent for a long while. She hesitantly reached out and touched the black handle of Smoke's sheathed Dao sword, jutting up over his shoulder.

"Can this sword-shadow… love? Can you love a human even though you're really a sword?" she asked. Her heart was pounding painfully in her chest.

"Of course I can, don't be silly," he said, smiling again. "I have emotions and needs just like you. I still have a human heart, even if I don't have a human soul. As I said, the projection is an exact replica of a living human being. May I ask why you ask this?"

"Um… Uh… N-no reason. Just c-curious." Neomi stammered, but she was blushing to the roots of her hair. *Smooth seducing, girl.* Well, unless the man was thick as a brick, he would know what was on her mind now, regardless of her clumsy delivery. Hopefully, it would only be a matter of time.

But hopefully not too much time at that. She had terminal cancer, and she knew now that Smoke was quite capable of perishing in the line of duty. She didn't have a lot of time to wait.

* * *

Misery

Neomi was in Math class, on a late Tuesday morning.

It had been a horrible, gut-wrenching day today. She was staring dully at the teacher writing on the blackboard up at the far front of the classroom, and she was trying to ignore her churning stomach. *Not gonna throw up. Not gonna throw up.* This was ridiculous. This whole day had been ridiculous, she had been having at least five convulsive power-puking fits every hour so far today; sometimes it happened as many as nine or even ten times an hour, which pretty much meant spending the whole hour throwing up nonstop. She was exhausted. It hadn't even been five minutes since the last explosive vomit session, she had to hold off another five minutes at least. *Not gonna throw up. Not gonna throw up.*

She was going to throw up. Right now.

Neomi just managed to turn her head in time to face the open rear door beside her, roaring flames bursting from her mouth as she lurched to her feet. She retched again, sending an even more powerful jet spraying out into the hallway to blacken the far wall. She doubled over clutching her belly as she vomited fire again and again, shooting out bigger and bigger fireblasts with each convulsive heave. Then with a supreme effort of will, she swallowed hard and clenched her teeth shut, and managed to get control of her stomach before it could turn to a full-power volcanic fit. She looked back at the class. Most everybody was staring at her, including the teacher. Well that was going to feed the rumour mill for a while. She mumbled "sorry, sorry," and slowly made her way out the door.

Not running. Running always made her vomit. She wouldn't make it ten yards if she ran. If she took her time, one slow plodding step after another, she at least had a chance to get to a window or something before the real eruption came out. *Not gonna throw up. Not gonna throw up.* She could do this.

Somehow, she got to the doors of the nearest stairwell safely. She was on the second floor of a three-story school building; should she go up to the roof or down and out to the parking lot? She decided on the roof again, as she'd been doing most of the day. She was so nauseous that her belly was glowing fiercely under her clothes; the next vomiting was going to be especially violent and she needed all the room she could get. It was more likely the light show would be seen from the ground, but at least she wouldn't incinerate any cars this way.

She made her way through the doors onto the landing, and encountered someone right there. A senior girl, leaning against the rail, boldly smoking a cigarette in the stairwell. What was this one's name, Allison? She hadn't seen this one for a long time, she might have transferred to another school and then transferred back in. Didn't matter, just another bully. She had ceased being afraid of bullies ever since she became a superhero. The smell of the tobacco smoke turned her stomach and she swallowed hard as burning bile surged up into her throat. *Not gonna throw up. Not gonna throw up.*

"Hey stunty." That was one of her many endearing nicknames from the bullies, this one referring to how tiny she was for her age. She plodded over to the stairs up, ignoring the older girl.

"Hey pizza-face, I'm talking to you!" Ah, the moniker about her acne. Instead of feeling hurt, she was more amused than anything. Her zits were long gone, her face smooth and angular. Getting called this particular nickname just made the caller look silly, and getting called at directly meant this bully obviously hadn't got the memo that Neomi was a superhero now. She trudged on.

A hand grabbed her shoulder. She was spun about, shoved against the wall. A sudden movement like this was very likely to make her vomit even when she wasn't feeling this sick, and she clenched her eyes shut and swallowed repeatedly to keep the rising bile down. *Not gonna throw up. Not gonna throw up.*

"I said I'm talking to you, bitch."

"You're really taking your life in your hands you know," Neomi said honestly, finally looking up and addressing the bully, who snorted with derisive amusement. "My name isn't 'bitch'. I'm the Volcano Girl. And right now I'm trying really hard not to burn you alive."

"You think I believe that crap? You can breathe fire? Don't make me laugh, dragon-girl. You're nothing but a lying little bitch."

"I'm not gonna say it again. Get out of my way or burn. I can't hold it in much longer."

"Go on then! Burn me!" The bully stepped back and threw her arms open. "I don't see no spray can, bitch! Fire away!"

You asked for it, idiot. The small girl opened her mouth, and relaxed her throat just a bit. The bile surged eagerly, and fire sprayed from her mouth. It was a bigger spurt of flame than she would have liked; the bully took it in the face, losing her eyebrows and her bangs. She hadn't actually wanted to hurt her, well not seriously anyway; she was a superhero, not a supervillain. The bully shrieked and flailed, jumping backwards and frantically batting at her head and clothes. Very satisfying.

"Holy s@#t!" the bully yelped, as the puff of fire dissipated and their eyes met. Neomi tried to speak, to say 'are you laughing now' or something smug like that, but more fire gushed out of her mouth again as soon as she opened it. The bully turned and fled down the hall. It was a good thing too; this spout of flame was much bigger and more powerful, chasing the bully down the hallway as the younger girl struggled to keep it from turning into a full-power killing blast. The fiery cloud dissipated revealing the bully smouldering but unharmed, still running, a fair distance away. Good. She wouldn't be trying any nonsense like that with her again and, hopefully, neither would her friends.

Neomi just barely managed to make it to the rooftop balcony before the flames started erupting full-force and out of control. She hunched over the rail, spewing titanic blasts of raging fire out over the canal at the back of the school, knees wobbling as her terrible power fully unleashed itself inside her petite body and exploded out through her small mouth. She was there for a long time, the fiery vomiting teasingly lessening in its violence and intensity till she thought it was about to stop before surging back to its full convulsive power, cycling over and over again. But it did end, eventually, and after a little time spent curled up on the floor panting for breath, she clambered to her feet feeling not so bad.

She had been using the roof as her primary vomit site for months. She had gotten skilled at aiming her flame-blasts upward over the dry canal into the empty sky rather than down into the canal directly, but the concrete ravine still looked like it was used as the launch platform for space rockets, wide swaths of it scorched black and cratered, some craters so deep that the foundation infrastructure underneath was exposed. The fire inside her was growing so powerful that it could destroy entire buildings when she vomited it out at full strength, she could only pray that she never lost control of it while she was still inside the school.

The small girl turned back toward the stairs… and her eyes met the shocked gaze of the two students not ten yards away. They were snuggled up against the elevator shack, a senior boy and a junior girl about her age, startled eyes wide open. Neomi noticed the pungent smell of their sweat and musk, saw that their clothes were all disheveled and half off, spotted the girl's panties lying a few feet away. It was a pair of lovers playing hooky, sneaking off to make out during class time. And they had just seen her whole fireblasting routine, right from the first retch.

They stared at each other for a long awkward moment. Then, blushing and feeling very self-conscious, Neomi abruptly put her fists on her hips and took a heroic pose, head held high with feet spread apart and chest outthrust.

"I'm Volcano Girl."

The junior raised her hand and made a quavering little wave hello. The senior just stared, his jaw slack and agape.

"Um... you probably shouldn't tell people about this," Neomi said after another long awkward pause. "They probably wouldn't believe you anyway."

They nodded quickly. She smelled the fear in their sweat now, replacing the musk of passion. The bitter scent turned her stomach, but not as much as the sadness that washed over her. Rather than a superhero, they saw something terrifying, even though they also saw her at her most vulnerable when she was exhausted. They saw a dragon perhaps, or some other fiery demonic monster in disguise. Burning bile rose in her throat. She suddenly needed to throw up again, right now, to get this awful sadness out of her.

"Excuse me," she gasped, and she rushed back to the railing as fire burst from her mouth again, blasting out over the charred canal like a volcanic geyser.

She was stuck there for another long harrowing session, gagging and gasping and choking as she vomited and vomited, and then when it was finally over she slumped to the floor once more, her back against the rail.

The couple was gone. They had left in such haste that the other girl had forgotten to pick up her undergarment on the way out, it was still laying there discarded on the floor. *Guess she's going commando for the rest of the day*, Neomi thought wryly.

The thought made her giggle. The Volcano Girl generally did not laugh. Laughing was one of the many, many things that made her inadvertently spout flames. But this time she just let it happen, just let the rhythmic spurts of fire from her stomach freely shoot up her throat and out her mouth as she laughed. Her stomach repeatedly flip-flopped in protest, the intense jolting nausea threatening to overwhelm her, but she didn't care. Laughter was a joy she rarely experienced. It felt so good that it was well worth the risk of yet another round of violent flame-vomiting to do it.

The doors to the stairwell opened beside her, and the vice-principal stepped out. Neomi gulped and stopped laughing, but her stomach kept flip-flopping inside her and she spouted fire twice again before she could get it under control. The vice-principal gazed at her with sympathetic eyes. He was an imposing man with salt-and-pepper brown hair and beard, but he had a soothing, soft deep voice. He also had a son with debilitating superhuman powers much like her, making him one of the few adults sympathetic to her plight.

"Having a bad day?"

Neomi didn't answer, just nodded as she pressed her hands to her churning tummy. She didn't feel like laughing any more. The vice-principal moved beside her, and squatted down to see eye-to-eye with her.

"You should have come to me sooner. It's getting hard to cover for you, Neomi. Quite a few people saw your fire-spitting act just now, and it wasn't easy to convince them you're just a compulsive pyro playing magic tricks."

Neomi nodded again contritely. The vice-principal sighed.

"You've only scorched some walls and a troublemaking bully today, so that's workable. Today so far, we've had an actual pyro, two kids bringing in guns, three incidents with drugs and one boy who actually assaulted a teacher, so a little graffiti burned away and a whining brat are the least of our troubles in comparison. But one of these days the principal is going to get tired of hearing your name and you'll end up suspended again or perhaps even expelled. You have to come to me when you're this sick, Miss Eid. We can't go on like this forever."

The girl just nodded again, gazing up at him with bleary eyes. He stood up and offered her a hand. She accepted and slowly got to her feet, but then she abruptly turned and threw herself half over the railing as fire exploded from her mouth yet again. The vice-principal kind-heartedly rubbed her heaving back as she gagged and retched and spewed colossal blasts of roaring flame into the canal. It took a long while, but when her fiery vomiting eventually eased up he spoke again.

"I can arrange for a bus to take you home. Or if you prefer, you can stay in the infirmary till school is finished, and I'll make sure you get the bed next to the window. Which do you want?"

Neomi didn't answer for a moment, panting over the railing as smoke billowed from her scorched mouth, then she eventually whispered: "I can't go home. My mother is home right now. Can I just sleep in the infirmary please?"

The vice-principal nodded and put a gentle arm around her delicate shoulders to usher her back toward the stairs. But this final gesture of compassion proved too much for her, and Neomi collapsed weeping into his arms. The man sighed again as he held the small girl, patting her back and stroking her hair as she quivered and sobbed wretchedly in his embrace. In this instance she wasn't a superhuman hero for justice anymore, just a very sick and very sad little girl.

It was going to be a long day for both of them.

* * *

Ambush

Neomi opened her eyes.

She was immensely disoriented. It was dark and cold, she smelled concrete and smog on the wind. She was horribly nauseous, so much so that the glow from her belly was shining through her sweater. She recognized that she was on the roof of her school, laying in foetal position on the rooftop balcony. The sky was dark, almost past sunset; the city-wide curfew would be in effect soon. How did she get here?

Memory slowly returned. She fainted, that's all. She had come up to the roof for a vomit session during the last class of the day, and she had power-puked so violently that she fainted afterward. That was all. She fainted and had been out for a couple hours, that was all.

Neomi pondered that as she got up and wearily bent over the railing again in preparation for the next vomiting. She wasn't prone to fainting. This was the second time though, last week she had fainted after a ferocious puke session much as she had just now. She hoped this wasn't going to become a regular occurrence. That would significantly cripple her usefulness as a superhero, right when she was at the cusp of becoming one.

Further introspection became impossible as her stomach suddenly turned over and the fire burst from her mouth. No matter how much she did it, she would never get used to it; it was always an ordeal even when it was a relatively mild attack. Gagging, choking, gasping for breath, great jets of fire forcing up her throat and out her small mouth so violently that her jaws were stretched wide open, body convulsing as though she was being kicked in the belly. It went on and on forever, and just when she thought it was finished it started up all over again. And again. And again.

She didn't faint again when it was finally over though. She didn't even collapse to the floor, she fell to her knees but gripped the rail and stayed upright with a supreme exertion of will. *If I'm going to be a superhero, I'll have to do better than this*, she thought. *If I keep training with Smoke, maybe someday soon I'll be able to stay standing after a long puke. Maybe someday I'll even be able to run again.*

After catching her breath, she got up and headed to the stairs at once. The night was full of roving gangs and worse as time went on, and the sun was almost gone already. She was a superhero now, it was her job to take out nighttime menaces, but the school was in an especially dangerous part of Meridian city and she wanted to be in her neighbourhood pronto. She couldn't take on the whole city. She could only protect her own territory and make the occasional raid outside. And having missed the school buses, she was a long way from her own territory.

As soon as she entered the stairwell, the pungent stink of marijuana smoke and Blue Angel taint assailed her senses. Her stomach flip-flopped and hot bile squirted up her throat, and she retched up a big gush of flames before she could stop herself. She went still. Had they heard her? No, she could hear the smokers talking; it sounded like they were at the bottom of the stairwell on the ground level. She carefully made her way down the stairs, moving silently, stalking them. Her enemies were near.

They did not spot her as she drew close to them and prepared to ambush. A couple of schoolgirls about her age and a tainted man in a trench coat. They were all smoking joints and the tainted one, the Legionnaire, was holding up a glowing gem-like blue marble for the girls to see: a Blue Angel pill. He already had them on the weed, now he was coaxing them to go deeper down the rabbit hole. *Oh no you don't.*

"Hey! Sto-*uuhh*!!" Neomi called out to them just as the Legion dealer was reaching out his blue-veined hand to give one of the girls the deadly pill, but unfortunately she spoke too forcefully for her stomach to handle, and fire surged up her throat and out her mouth as she doubled over retching. The three reacted to the sudden appearance of a flame-spewing girl as one might expect: they turned and ran.

The Legionnaire stepped backward out the double doors and disappeared out into the parking lot. The two girls unwisely tried to flee deeper into the school building, only to find the inner doors locked as they always were for the night. They whirled about and faced Neomi with terrified eyes as she threw up gush after gush of billowing flames toward them. She managed to regain control of herself before the flame spouts grew large enough to reach the girls, and she straightened up and regarded them. Taking a deep breath, she put her fists on her hips and took a heroic pose, and got into character.

"I'm Volcano Girl," she said boldly. "And you're breaking the law. I don't care about the weed. But you can't have the pills."

The small girl turned her gaze toward the glowing Blue Angel pill where it had fallen. She pointed at it. "That thing will do worse than kill you. It's not like other drugs. It's evil. It will turn you into monsters. Don't you ever touch this stuff."

With that, Neomi opened her mouth and shot out a stream of flame over the pill. It popped and scattered glimmering fluid about before it all evaporated into nothingness. With some effort she swallowed down the fiery stream then turned her gaze back to the schoolgirls, and she noticed that they smelled of expensive perfume and were wearing expensive clothing.

"You can call a cab to take you home?" she asked. A taxi in this city was a luxury that few schoolkids could afford; these looked like upper-class kids who could. The girls nodded cautiously.

"Then go home. And I better not catch you doing this again, or you'll regret it. Now go!"

The two girls were quick to obey, and dashed for the doors.

"Remember!" Neomi called out after them. "I'm Volcano G-*uuhh*!!"

She doubled over retching again, spewing flames all over the landing. *Well that's embarrassing.* She really needed to be more careful on how loudly she spoke, whether giving a superhero speech or not.

It took a while to regain control of her rebellious stomach. The landing's walls, railings, steps, doors and entire floor space were all blackened and scorched by her fiery vomiting by the time she was able to stop. She was very lucky that the vomiting hadn't progressed to a full strength power-puking fit that would have destroyed the landing entirely. That was enough damage to school property for the day, thank you. She straightened up and cautiously rubbed her glowing tummy, then opened the fire-seared outer door and looked out. She was horrified to see that night had fallen, that the sunset was just a fading glow in the western sky. Her mentor Smoke hadn't come looking for her so he was likely on a mission, hence it was going to be a long, dangerous walk alone through the dark to get home.

She rushed out to the parking lot, moving as swiftly on her feet as she dared. Running made her vomit, and even walking too fast could set her off. One measured step after another, she hurried through the parking lot, trying not to gag from the stink of car engine oil and gasoline. Across the lot onto the far road she went, down the street and into the district's concrete jungle of ruined structures and empty buildings and dark alleys. It was another lightless night, choked with smog and illuminated only by the ghostly streetlamps, and a pervading feeling of dread began to overshadow her perpetual nausea.

Periodically the young girl was forced to halt, gripping her belly and throwing up blazing streams of fire when her quick pace became too much for her churning stomach, but at least it didn't progress into the convulsive volcanic vomiting that could decimate whole streets and take ages to stop. Her fiery displays were a bright beacon to anyone or anything lurking in the dark from one end of the street to the other, but what choice did she have? It was either move quick and visible, or slow and vulnerable. She could only hope that any that saw her would be reluctant to engage a passerby apparently armed with a flamethrower at the ready.

Abruptly she stopped. Neomi smelled something over the nauseating everyday-odors of the inner city streets. It was the Blue Angel taint she smelled, the intensely sickening stink of a body extensively mutated by the virulent drug. As she doubled over vomiting fire again she realized it wasn't just any body she smelled, it was the Legion dealer she had just encountered at school. He had passed this way recently. He was close. She regained control of her stomach after a moment and looked around warily and fearfully. She was between streetlamps right now and could barely see anything in the dark.

Taking a deep breath, she opened her mouth just a bit and carefully retched. The fire eagerly surged up from her stomach and shot out her mouth in a narrow jet like the stream from a water hose, one of the techniques she had discovered through Smoke's training. At first the stream was far more powerful than what she wanted, wrenching her jaws open and shooting out a good twenty yards down the street like a firehose jet. With effort, she narrowed the 'O' orifice formed by her lips and constricted her throat and stomach, and the stream dwindled in length and force till it was just a single yard long, like a bright blade of flame.

The blade radiantly illuminated the area around her, much better than a handheld burning torch could do. Her visibility was somewhat impaired by the flickering tongues of fire rising in front of her eyes, and she had to hold her breath while her stomach continuously vented its flames out through her mouth, but now she could see quite effectively in the dark.

Now armed with her flame blade, Neomi made her way down the street. Shadows flickered in the alleys and doorways and behind every intervening piece of architecture or rubble, and she nervously turned her face to keep the blade pointed at any potential source of danger. Periodically she turned to check behind her, to make sure she wasn't followed. At the next streetlamp she closed her mouth and swallowed down the stream of fire while she caught her breath. She could still smell the dealer, and worse, she could now smell other tainted bodies with him. Her trek was growing more and more dangerous with every step. But what choice did she have?

She took a deep breath, retched up another flame blade, and advanced into the darkness beyond the safe ring of lamplight. Then things started to happen.

A glimmer of light off to one side, firelight reflecting on metal flying through the air toward her. Acting on well-trained reflex, Neomi instinctively turned her head to point her mouth at the spinning knife and expelled a sharp blast of searing flame that subsumed her fiery blade, and the knife instantly shattered and disintegrated as it entered the roiling cloud. She was being attacked!

Another movement, on the other side of the street. There was a loud bang sound, the light of a muzzle flash. Scarcely aware of what she was doing, the small girl whipped her head around to aim her mouth toward the incoming threat and intensified the blast of shielding fire she was spewing forth, and the leaden bullet vaporized in a tiny streak of black smoke piercing partway through the cloud. Several more pistol reports followed, and several more bullets futilely pierced the flaming barrier and did not penetrate through.

More movement in the shadows, on either side and before her. Dark rangy blue-veined bodies charging toward her, firelight glinting off fanged teeth and knife blades. This was a trap, a prepared Legion ambush, and she had walked right into it. Cold fear and hot hatred ran through her, vying for dominion.

Neomi had just about had enough. As harrowing as they were, she had dealt with such ambushes before. *I'm the Volcano Girl, scum. You just picked the wrong fight.* She opened her mouth as wide as it would go, and stopped resisting the nausea completely. Her stomach somersaulted joyfully, raging flame exploding up her throat and out her mouth in a cataclysmic inferno-blast that deluged the entire street. She turned her head from side to side and then turned around to cover the rear arc, tearing up the road, collapsing the buildings on either side of the street, disintegrating hollowed-out cars and streetlamps and any possible cover from the fiery devastation she had unleashed. She was vaguely aware of tall dark bodies around her, of knives swooping and pistols barking, just for fleeting instants before everything turned to smoke and ash and bone. Nothing could stand before the might of the Volcano Girl's flame.

Her stomach continued venting the titanic flame-geyser out through her mouth for one endless minute before she managed to choke it back down and swallow it. Unleashing a blast like that would have overwhelmed her not that long ago, sending her into a fit of convulsive vomiting that would have taken ages to stop and left her exhausted and helpless. But she had gained a measure of hard-earned self-control from her training, and she called on it now to tame the inferno within. Her stomach seethed with churning fury; she had only deferred the full-strength eruption, not quelled it. But she was well on her way to becoming a fully trained and battle-hardened superhero. She could partially control her power now, she was not completely at the mercy of it.

It seemed as though the battle was over. But Neomi could still smell Angel-tainted flesh over the sterile smell of the smoke and ash… behind her. Panicking, she whirled around, spewing clouds of flames over… an empty street. No one there. But she could smell them somewhere. There were dark windows and doors looming open, open alleys and cars to hide behind. They could be lurking anywhere, ready to come at her from any direction. She was out in the open and vulnerable. What would her mentor Smoke do if he was here?

He… would go somewhere unexpected. Somewhere the Legionnaires couldn't have planned for. She cast her eyes about, and realized there was a building right beside her that hadn't collapsed from the force of her flame; this building had no open windows and its door was chained shut. There couldn't possibly be any of them in there. She turned and forcefully retched at the building, streaking fireballs flying from her mouth with each retch to detonate against the front of the structure like grenades, smashing through the wall in seconds. Several fiery projectiles later, a dark, empty space loomed before her.

Then Neomi rushed for it, moving as fast as she dared. She moved too fast; fire burst from her mouth again as her volatile stomach revolted against the jolts of her footsteps. But she just gripped her belly and kept on going, lurching forward step by step while she hunched forward and continuously spewed streams of flame over the ground in front of her. When she reached the opening she made good use of her involuntary expulsion, sweeping the burning flow back and forth to illuminate the darkened building and clear it of any hostiles. It would seem there were none, nothing that she could see anyway. With effort she managed to choke down and swallow the spurting fire, and she hurried inside. She smelled only musty air and dust over the smoke of her own flames, giving her a measure of relief that she was alone.

The girl turned and looked back at the large opening smashed through the wall that she had just come through. This would be the only immediate way to get into this building now, and she could deal with that. Gripping her middle, Neomi panted for breath as her nausea surged and the fiery glow in her belly changed to a deep crimson-red, then she abruptly doubled over vomiting a heavy stream of gluey liquid Magmite over the flooring in front of her. She turned her head and passed the stream side to side, liberally coating the floor around the opening, and sheets of fire flared up as the viscous blazing lava ignited on contact with the air, barring the entrance with a literal wall of flame.

It took a precious minute to stop throwing up the Magmite lava, but she eventually forced herself to cease, and the crimson glow in her belly returned to its normal fiery orange-yellow. She turned and hurried deeper into the building, retching up a flame blade to light her passage. This had only bought her some time, now she needed to escape.

After some exploration, she found a rear door. But this potential means of escape had a sturdy obstacle: a metal door barred and chained shut presumably on both sides. The last owners of the building had been very particular about its security, it seemed. This obstacle wouldn't stop her for long, but the thought occurred to her that she shouldn't simply smash through the door with a power-blast. If she could escape through the rear of the building without making a lot of noise, that might give her a chance to elude the Legionnaires on the street completely.

Neomi swallowed her flame blade and took a deep breath, gripping her tummy and gagging repeatedly as the fiery glow in her belly turned to a pulsating green light, then she doubled over vomiting out the strange green-white goo that Smoke called 'Plasma,' spraying the searing firestuff all over the heavy metal door. The thick goo was so hot that it instantly melted through the metal like a powerful acid, and then evaporated within seconds, leaving nothing but a steaming cavity over a molten pool. There was nothing of the seething roar that accompanied her other fireblasts, only a faint sizzling barely audible over Neomi's noisy gagging and retching. It took another vital minute to stop throwing up the Plasma, but the instant she was able to walk again she was on the move, stepping over the puddle of liquid metal out into the back alley. She smelled no taint here, only dust, concrete, and ancient garbage besides the metal vapor-scent. She didn't hesitate, hurrying on her way deeper into the alley network as quickly as she could. She did not encounter the Legionnaires again; she had escaped their ambush and was finally on her way home again.

It was only till Neomi was a long way away from that particular street did she stop to catch her breath, and the green glow in her belly returned to its normal fiery colour. She seated herself on a broken bus stop bench and relaxed a moment, trying to ignore the raging nausea that threatened to overwhelm her any moment now, and smiled a little smile. A pat on the back was in order. She had survived a deadly Legion ambush and come out of it with most of her enemies defeated. The drug dealer was very likely one of the Legionnaires she had immolated; he would spread no Angel-taint among her schoolmates any more. Tonight, the Volcano Girl was triumphant.

The small girl abruptly raised her fist high, throwing her head back and letting out a cry of victory. Her stomach vengefully erupted through her mouth at once, sending a gigantic roaring fountain of flame shooting into the night sky, and she just let it happen, allowing the geyser of fire to vent freely out her mouth as she cried out a long, distorted *"Yeeaah!!"* as loudly as she possibly could. The fire wouldn't stop coming out when she finished her shout, souring her exultation somewhat as she was forced to double over vomiting the flames all over the street, but the feeling remained. Nothing could take that wonderful feeling from her.

Somehow, she made it home. It took hours, one plodding step after another with her blade of flame always streaming from her mouth to light the darkness, while explosive power-puking fits regularly drove her to her knees and devastated her surroundings. Neomi's stomach was incensed by the extensive harnessing of its power tonight and was intent on venting out more flames than she could possibly control, and she spent much more time on her knees vomiting her fiery guts out than she did on her feet. She was accosted again once, by a gang of untainted street hoodlums, but a few massive blasts of fire from her mouth scared them off without her having to burn anybody. The Volcano Girl never killed humans if she didn't have to.

There were only a few hours left in the night by the time she eventually made it through the dark city back to her own neighbourhood. Her parents were in bed when she got home, and they mercifully did not investigate the sound of her uncontrollable vomiting in the ruins of the upstairs bathroom. After a shower and another furiously violent puke session, she crawled into her own bed without trying to force herself to eat anything, and did her best to sleep and recover her strength in the brief periods between the intense vomiting fits. She couldn't wait to share her exploits with her friend and mentor tomorrow. She was another step closer to becoming a true superhero now.

Tonight, the Volcano Girl was triumphant.

* * *

Clash

Neomi stood with the superhuman hero Smoke on the roof of the abandoned warehouse, watching out into the night. Smoke was her mentor, her friend, and tonight, her partner The grey-clad sword-bearing warrior stared toward the distant dark warehouse, twin to this building, which was very much not abandoned. This was to be their target tonight: a Legion production and distribution hub of the dread Blue Angel pills. And it was also to be the focus of Neomi's final trial, the proving ground where she would become a true superhero.

"What can you see?" Neomi asked her mentor worriedly; she knew he could see in the dark. "Am I allowed to ask that?"

"This isn't an exam, Miss Volcano Girl," he answered, his tone calm and focused. "We are partners in this mission, and all my knowledge and powers are yours as you need them. I just want you to take the lead because this is a seek-and-destroy job, and your powers of destruction outmatch me by far. The only one who is testing you is yourself."

"Okay," said Neomi timidly. She took a deep breath and steeled herself, unconsciously assuming her 'super pose' with fists on hips, feet spread apart and chest outthrust. "Superhero Smoke. Tell me what you can see."

"I see one very large main building, large enough to take heavy transports and construction equipment," he reported. "I see a number of small satellite buildings in the yard, along with many shipping containers. Six transport trucks are parked in the side parking lot without any containers attached. The hangar doors facing the yard are closed, and all the forklifts and other utility vehicles are parked. There is a guard tower, but I don't see any watchmen. In fact I don't see any movement in the compound at all."

"No movement at all?" Neomi queried. "Are you sure this is a Legion drug lab? It sounds deserted."

"I was sure as of two days ago," he confirmed. "Unless they have evacuated everything in the last 48 hours, this is still our primary target for this district."

"Okay... well I guess I could burn up the whole warehouse from outside if you watch my back," said Neomi. "Should we do that?"

"It is a valid course of action. But this is an unsubtle and imprudent approach. Any useful items or innocent prisoners inside would perish. It would create a big light-show that would attract attention from the surrounding areas. And such strenuous use of your power could send it out of control, which would effectively incapacitate you. I would not recommend this strategy."

"Okay. Well... what would you recommend?"

"We should clear the watchtower first. I may not have seen them, but there could be sentries on guard. Then we check the outer buildings, then enter the warehouse from the side, engaging any targets of opportunity as we encounter them. And we should stay together. Either of us could handle one or two Legionnaires on our own, but more than that and we risk being pinned down while one of them radios for help."

"Okay. Okay," said Neomi, taking a deep breath and trying to focus herself. Her stomach roiled with anxiety and excitement, and she tried to calm herself.

"Let's teleport right into the watchtower and ambush anybody in there," she ordered. "Then we'll circle the compound on foot to clear the outside buildings, and then we'll find a way inside the warehouse and finish the job. You'll take point and sneak ahead, and I'll back you up with my fire if we run into trouble. But listen, you know the fire is always building up inside me. I puked it out as hard as I could before you picked me up, so we've got maybe an hour before I have to vomit at full strength again. That means we need to finish this well before midnight. Okay?"

Some things never changed. Even though she was on the cusp of superheroism, even though her self-control had actually improved despite her power having grown tenfold, she still had to vomit forth her devastating full-strength power puke at least once an hour every hour of the day and night. Try as she might to hold it back, regardless of how much she emptied her stomach beforehand, it was evident that there was simply nothing she could do about that inescapable hourly puke. That was just the way it was, and she had no choice but to plan her life and her mission around it.

"Very good, Miss Volcano Girl," Smoke affirmed. "I'm ready."

"All right, let's go!" she exclaimed, channeling her Paragon comic heroes' enthusiasm. "Time to rock and r-*uuhh*!!"

Unfortunately, she got a little too enthusiastic. Hot bile surged up her throat from her excited stomach and she doubled over retching as flames sprayed out from her mouth. *Oops!* Not a very auspicious start. Smoke quickly called forth a thick wall of his smoke with a wave of his arm, obscuring the worst of the fiery light, hopefully keeping it from attracting the attention of anyone at the distant Legion base. Then he moved beside Neomi, gently rubbing her back as she threw up gush after gush of blazing flames into the night.

It took a few minutes, but with a mighty exertion of will she eventually clenched her teeth shut and swallowed down the spouting flames, gaining control of herself before the vomiting could grow any more violent. She straightened up and wiped the ash from her lips, blushing deeply.

"Oh gosh, I'm sorry," she said, panting for breath, embarrassed beyond words. "I'm so keyed up… I just… I just sort of-*uuhh*!!"

"Calm yourself, Neomi," her mentor urged her, continuing to rub her back as she doubled over spewing out big gushes of flame again. "You're not a novice any more. Your training is complete, you're an experienced superhero now. You can control it. You know you can."

His words and his cool ashen scent were so soothing that her stomach started to settle down at once. The young girl steeled herself, and after another minute or so she managed to stop throwing up the flames. She straightened up and cautiously rubbed her glowing belly. Her volatile stomach squirted burning bile up her throat one last time and made her retch out a final fiery spout, and then she was calm and composed once more. She stood up straight and took a deep breath.

"Okay. Okay. I'm good," she said brusquely, turning to face Smoke. "My stomach is being a real bitch tonight, but I'm on top of it now."

"Are you ready then?" he asked, his demeanor imperturbable as he allowed his mist-wall to dissipate.

"Ready. Let's do this."

"Very good, Miss Volcano Girl."

The two superheroes moved to stand back-to-back.

Smoke drew his black Dao sword. Neomi's belly flared with fiery light. Then Smoke's cool white smoke rose up all around them, and suddenly they were... somewhere else.

Neomi smelled the Legionnaires' sickening alien scent long before she could see them through the mist. There was one right in front of her and one on her left side, and more were behind her facing Smoke. Raging flames instantly exploded from her mouth before she could think, and as the mist vanished she saw the altered ganger in front of her perish in a spray of black ash and charred fragments of bone.

Everything was happening around her in a blur of speed. To the rear, Smoke had sprang toward the unseen adversaries behind her, and there was the swish of a whirling sword and the meaty impacts of a body and its severed head hitting the metal floor. To her side, the other Angel-tainted thug had his back turned to them, but he was spinning around and drawing his sidearm quick as a flash. Barely aware of what she was doing, Neomi turned and violently retched fire at the deformed ganger before he could bring his weapon to bear, and he too disappeared in a flying spray of ash and fragmented bone.

And just like that, the ambush was over. Neomi turned and saw that Smoke had dispatched a fourth Legionnaire, and they were sharing the rickety watchtower with only ash and bloody corpses now. The superhuman warrior swiftly looked one way and the next to see if they had been spotted. Below, the open yard of the shipping compound was darkened and silent: it would seem that they were as yet undetected. He flicked the blue-glowing blood droplets from his black blade and sheathed it, and she struggled not to gag at the stench of the tainted blood.

"Clear," he reported, speaking just loud enough for Neomi to hear. A shuddering thrill ran through her body. The mission had begun. They were in the danger zone now, in enemy territory, on the clock. And they had already drawn blood. The killing of Angel-tainted Legionnaires had become almost rote for her, but it still disquieted her: even if they were her enemy, even if they would kill her without hesitation, they had still been human once.

With her flames dissipating, the girl could barely see a thing within the unlit interior of the watchtower. Her belly's fiery glow briefly turned to a deep red and she retched out a fat spout of sizzling gooey Magmite, which splattered over the floor and sent up a small column of crimson fire. With the watchtower illuminated by the Magmite flare she could see now that there was a mounted machinegun affixed on the railing, angled to cover almost the entirety of the compound. This was a threat they could not ignore, a weapon that could be turned on them while they were searching the grounds. Smoke was inspecting it. As she watched on, the warrior unloaded the belt-fed weapon and closed off the munitions case beside it, and he beckoned her over.

"Melt the feed tray of the gun and the hinges of the ammo box," he instructed her. "Make it look like there's nothing wrong, but be careful not to set off the rounds inside the box. Can you do that?"

Neomi wordlessly opened her mouth and shot a narrow stream of flame onto the gun, and then on the case as directed, carefully disabling the emplacement without complication. Small expulsions like this were easier to control, it was the big blasts that were wont to set off her stomach. Smoke stood at the railing and kept watch while she worked, watching for any below who might notice the light from her flame. She was growing even more anxious, and her belly's light flared in nervous response as the fire streaming from her mouth grew bright and intense.

With that potential threat taken care of, she turned her attention to the open trapdoor and ladder in the center of the tower floor. Smoke held out his hand to her, offering to teleport her down. But the girl just swallowed her flame stream and walked right past him as she went straight for the ladder. Her mentor stared in surprise; he knew that she couldn't climb without throwing up.

"I've got this," Neomi whispered tersely. "Get down there and scout out the area. I'll be right down."

The warrior looked at her curiously but didn't argue, and he hopped over the railing forthwith, dropping some forty feet straight down to land in a crouch silently and unharmed at the base of the watchtower. Steeling herself, the young superheroine mounted the ladder and began climbing down. She wanted to do this, to prove herself, even if she was the only one keeping score.

Her nausea soared as she descended, her stomach forcibly spouting burning bile up her throat with each jarring step onto each rung, but she didn't try to fight it. She just turned her face to the side and allowed the rhythmic spurts of flame to shoot out from her open mouth as she climbed, but she did so in a controlled fashion, letting the gushes of fire vent out from her stomach in a steady even rhythm while firmly restraining them from growing in size or intensity. She was very anxious, and so her flames were bright and hot, but the blasts never grew any larger than the size of a small vehicle and passed harmlessly between the struts of the tower. The light would be seen if there was anyone out there of course, but that was to be expected. Any operation involving the Volcano Girl could only expect limited stealth anyway; the plan would be to quickly neutralize any who might notice her, not hide from them indefinitely.

Smoke was waiting for her at the bottom. He was halfway between the tower and the closest building, crouching beside a metal trucking container. He changed position a bit so she could see him clearly in the moonlight and made the hand signal for 'area clear,' then waved her over. She held position for a minute, hunched over and spewing jets of flame over the ground while she waited for the fiery vomiting to stop, then she moved to him, crossing the open ground as quickly as her stomach would tolerate.

"Still no visible activity," her partner reported as she came up beside him. "But I can see light coming from under the main doors. And I'm hearing a sound I can't place, a sort of whirring or humming. That's not coming from the main building but around the side. Instructions?"

"Uh, what about this thing? What's in it?" asked Neomi, pointing to the shipping container beside them. She mostly smelled metal corrosion and rust from it, but there was also an odd waxy scent that turned her stomach much more than the dank rust.

"A good question. The hatch is barred with a padlock. Shall I bring out my lockpicks?"

The girl could tell that her partner was smiling under his ninja-style mask. She gave him a dry look.

Stepping around the corner to the rear of the container, she located the padlock and carefully retched fire on it, liquefying the lock in seconds. The blob of molten metal plopped to the ground, and she cautiously pulled the hatch open. The interior was filled with locked metal crates; another fiery retch melted one of the locks and she lifted the lid of the crate.

"Those are the shells of the blue pills," the warrior confirmed as she lifted up a handful of empty gel spheres for him to see. "They deteriorate if they aren't filled within a matter of days, so we're definitely at the right place."

Smoke proceeded onward, scouting further ahead of her while she watched on and covered him. Before she left to join him, Neomi took a breath and vomited a heavy sustained blast of fire into the container, quickly turning all the metal crates within into slag. It might have been a meaningless gesture given all the other shipping containers in the yard, but she wasn't going to let any opportunity to hurt the Legion go to waste.

They moved around the corner of the main warehouse building. This was the side lot of the compound, with a couple of trucks and several satellite buildings as well as a large and obvious secondary entrance to the main warehouse. There was a security shack at the main gate where a guard was meant to monitor and allow passage in and out of the compound, but large glass windows made it appear that the small hut was empty.

She decided to investigate the security hut first, and pointed at it to make her partner aware of her intent. The superhero nodded and promptly dissolved into grey smoke. A moment passed, then the door of the shack opened, and Smoke took a step out and waved her over. The girl flinched a little when she stepped inside; the hut had in fact been manned, and the Legion guard's body was on the floor with its severed head fallen a distance away. Smoke flicked the glowing blue blood from his blade and sheathed it, and he moved to take watch while she searched the interior.

Neomi discovered a number of items of interest: an unlocked lockbox packed full of cash and Blue Angel pills (she confiscated the money and retched fire on the pills), the control panel for opening and closing the main gate (she retched fire on the controls to ensure the open gate could never be closed), an armoury locker full of large blades and firearms (she retched fire into it and destroyed the weapons), a key cupboard with a variety of vehicle keys and door keycards (she claimed the master keycard and retched fire on the rest), an empty holding cell for prisoners (she retched fire on it and melted all the bars), and a camera system monitoring several areas of the outer compound (she checked for any activity and then retched fire all over the bank of monitors). Smoke watched on as she plundered and ravaged the building, and shook his head when she triumphantly offered him the master keycard and cash.

"I have no need of them. Besides, you're in charge. You get first pick of anything useful we find."

The young girl was a bit flabbergasted, as the amount of currency was more than she had ever seen in her life. She pocketed the loot with a dazed smile, and the duo proceeded out of the smouldering shack and onward.

They investigated the satellite buildings next: two were obviously garages for the servicing of the vehicles in the parking lot, the other ten or so turned out to be storage shacks with a variety of tools and supplies. Neomi vomited a torrent of flames into each of the twelve buildings, destroying everything inside, then she vomited into the cabins of the six trucks. By now they had done some significant damage to the Legion facility, and their mission wasn't even halfway finished. But afterward, after she had finished disabling the last truck, her partner watched on with concern as she hunched over and groaned in discomfort, gripping her blazing-bright belly as thick smoke billowed from her mouth.

"How long?" he asked. He didn't need to say more. They were both well aware that it was only a matter of time before Neomi's stomach would erupt out through her mouth at full power, and all this deliberate flame-vomiting was obviously aggravating it rather than relieving it.

"Twenty minutes maybe, half an hour at most," she panted. She managed a smile. "Don't worry Zhen, we'll be done long before that."

"Very good, Miss Volcano Girl."

It was time for their primary objective. They moved toward the side entrance of the giant warehouse, staying close to the wall. The personnel entry was through a large pair of wide-open doors, inside which there appeared to be a deep dark hallway.

Neomi could smell something strange, a warm sweetness that smelled distinctly like honey, but merged and mingled with the alien sickly-sweetness of Blue Angel taint. Smoke halted ahead of her and held up a hand. She could hear it now, a low humming, buzzing sound.

"Thought so. Altered bees," her partner murmured "Fed with Angel essence. They're triple-sized and vicious, and they only attack the untainted. Sounds like there's a big hive just inside the hall. We've got problems."

"Why? Can they affect you?"

"Yes. Their venom can infect my ghost form, just like Angel-poisoned knives can. Your power is ideal against them, but you'll have to take them all out quickly. They move very fast when they're swarming. And if they…"

Whatever he was about to say was abruptly interrupted as a hideous, blue-glowing, fist-sized insect flitted out of the open doorway, passing right by him as it came straight towards Neomi. The girl let out a yelp of fright and fire sprayed from her mouth, turning the giant bug to a burning cinder that plummeted to the ground and came apart. The droning buzz from inside the doors faded to silence for a few chilling seconds. Then the buzzing started again, now deep and menacing and loud as an airplane's propeller.

"Move! Hurry!" Smoke barked, and he grabbed her shoulders and rushed her to the doorway. Still spewing flames, the girl stumbled into the darkened hallway. Inside, she saw a great misshapen mass in the far corner of the hall, and a swirling, terrifying cloud of lights like blue-glowing fireflies flying straight at her. A mighty geyser of fire instantly exploded from her mouth, thundering through the hallway and immolating everything within, incinerating the swarming cloud and the huge hive, and smashing through both side walls and the roof and far doors as well.

Her partner was behind her, holding her shoulders and walking her down the hallway as she hunched forward and clutched at her blazing-bright belly, blast after gigantic blast erupting from her mouth into the building and wreaking havoc on everything before her. Unbeknownst to her, the few altered bees wandering the grounds outside were zooming back to their ruined hive, flying into the hallway behind the two superheroes and shooting toward them like glowing bullets. Smoke spun around to put his back to hers, whipping out his black sword and swinging at the incoming bees in a blinding-fast flurry of strikes, gracefully cutting the glowing missiles from the air like some implacable Jedi Knight. The infiltration phase was over, like it or not, and it was time for the frontal assault.

Neomi managed to choke down the gushing fire and swallow it after a time, and she continued to advance into the dark building, picking her way through the burning rubble and onward down the cratered floor. She couldn't see much in the dark and smoke, but there was much that she could hear and smell. A fire alarm klaxon was blaring now. She could hear angry shouts coming from deeper in the building, and she heard her own hero-name, "Volcano Girl," amidst the shouting. She detected a strong smell of Angel-tainted flesh wafting from ahead, amidst all the smoke and ash. And there was something else… the scent of normal human skin and perspiration, infused with the reek of fear.

"Smoke! They've got prisoners in here! I can smell them!" she exclaimed, as loudly as she dared.

"Then follow your nose! We've got to reach them before the Legionnaires start executing them!" Smoke answered. It seemed that the last of the fierce altered bees had been dispatched, and he turned his attention to the task ahead.

The duo rushed down the hall and into the warehouse proper, moving as fast as Neomi could safely walk; they were now in the small office complex of the personnel area. The giant work area, where the vehicles, stores and processing machinery would be, laid ahead. They reached the intersection at the end of the entrance hall… and almost ran into a team of Legionnaires who were charging down the side corridor toward the disturbance.

Fire immediately burst from the girl's mouth before she could think, a great blast that surged down the middle of the corridor and vaporized most of the altered gangers in an instant. Some were faster than she was, two of them diving through doorways on either side to escape the flames, one jumping up over the blast to come plummeting down with a machete held blade-first to impale her. Smoke was faster still: he leapt up to meet the aerial goon's charge, his black sword arcing upward to separate the Legionnaire from his weapon and his arm, followed up with a spectacular rising somersault kick that knocked the maimed ganger backwards down the corridor and into Neomi's raging flame torrent.

Neomi turned her erupting stream toward the open doorway where one of the Legion thugs had dived into, filling the office with flame and disintegrating everything within. Her partner landed facing the other doorway, only to catch a glimpse of the remaining ganger racing headlong away from them, smashing through the far door of the filing room beyond and retreating out of sight.

"Let him go! Keep looking for the prisoners!" Smoke ordered. With great effort Neomi swallowed down the blasting flow of flame and snapped her mouth shut. Now that she could breathe, she sniffed the air, trying not to gag from the stench of Legionnaire blood and burnt flesh. The scent of humans was coming from the opposite direction, the way that the Legion team had been running toward. Without a word she turned about and walked briskly down the corridor, fast as her volatile stomach would allow. Her mentor followed.

Moments later, the heavy metal door to the detainment area dissolved under the gushing firehose-fountain of molten green-white Plasma from Neomi's mouth. Smoke charged straight in while the girl struggled to stop vomiting up the Plasma, and several lightning-fast sword strikes later the three prison guards within were defeated. The prison was a small storage area with several heavy portable cells, all made of heavy-duty plexiglass, all locked with a keypad and card swipe. There were three to four human prisoners in each cubical cell, mostly young women; the Legion preferred to forcibly mutate and recruit captured males, while the unfortunate females were sold into slavery. The superhuman warrior quickly checked to make sure that the area was secure and the prisoners unharmed while his partner regained control of her stomach.

"Area secure," Smoke reported when the girl eventually entered the room. Noticing the control panels on the cells, Neomi quickly took out the master keycard she had claimed earlier on and swiped the closest panel. She hissed with disappointment as the keypad lit up while the cell door remained closed.

"It's code-locked," said her partner, taking a closer look. "I can see the fingerprints on the keys, give me a second."
The warrior typed in a sequence, then another, while the women inside the cell watched on hopefully.

"I know which keys were pressed, just not the order," he muttered as he worked. "Come on... almost there..."

"This is taking too long," Neomi snapped. "We don't have time to do this for every cell. Stand back everyone!"

The girl's belly was still glowing with a pulsating green hue. Taking a deep breath, Neomi opened her mouth and vomited a heavy stream of searing Plasma onto the prison cell before her, thoroughly bathing the plexiglass wall with the thick goo and melting it away in seconds. She walked sideways down the central corridor of the detainment area while continuously spouting out the Plasma, dissolving the front of each cell in turn. And when she reached the end of the corridor she turned the stream onto the outer wall, swiftly burning through the metal to produce a large gaping passage to the outside compound. It took her another few minutes to stop throwing up the molten goo, everyone watching on as she hunched over and spewed endless streams of the green-glowing firestuff out the dark hole; when she eventually finished and caught her breath, she poked her head out the hole to survey the area.

"Looks clear," she said after a moment, and turned to the women exiting the cells. "The gate is straight that-a-way. I'm sorry we can't go with you, but we have to shut down this warehouse."

"Don't worry, Volcano Girl. We can take care of ourselves," said the young lady closest to her. Neomi noticed that the freed prisoners had armed themselves with the deceased guards' weapons; three rifles, three sidearms and three machetes split amongst the twenty women. She permitted herself a proud smile that these unfamiliar women could identify her by name.

"Thank you Smoke! Thank you Volcano Girl!" said several of the others gladly, as they exited. "Go make those assholes pay!"

Neomi stayed at the breach in the wall while the women clambered over the melted trench outside the breach and ran across the grounds, her belly's glow returning to its usual fiery yellow-orange hue as she watched them go, and she kept an eye on them until they vanished out the open gate. Smoke stood on guard outside the melted door to the prison area. Just as the last of the prisoners escaped the girl heard the sounds of battle from outside the door: enraged shouting, grunts of exertion and pain, the clash of blades striking together, the crack of firearms discharging. She smelled gunpowder-smoke and Angel-tainted blood. Her heart pounding and her stomach churning, she rushed to render aid to her companion.

"Hang on Smoke! I'm com-*uuhh*!!"

Oops. Somewhere between speaking too loudly and stepping too fast, Neomi's stomach revolted and she doubled over gushing a fountain of flames from her mouth. *No way. Not this time.* She would be damned if she would let her miserable nausea get in the way of rescuing her partner from trouble. The girl lurched forward, gripping her belly and running onward on wobbly legs as she continued violently vomiting fire on the floor in front of her. She was vomiting so hard that the flame-stream was ripping up the floor before her, forcing her to stagger through a smouldering trench of her own making, but she determinedly pushed on.

When she got through the melted security door, she blurrily saw that Smoke had engaged three Legion thugs simultaneously, moving in a deadly dance of whirling steel as his sword clashed against the enemies' machetes. Two blue-bleeding bodies laid unmoving on the floor, a grim testament to the superhuman warrior's fighting skill, but the three he was currently battling were skilled enough to prove his match, and he was being steadily pushed back by their combined assault. In a split second Neomi realized that the blade-edges of the Legionnaires' machetes were glowing faintly blue, and she could smell the oily Blue Angel essence corroding the steel. Smoke's ghost-form manoeuvres were useless against the touch of these poisoned blades, and in these close quarters, he was in big trouble.

Even as she was throwing up her fiery guts, Neomi did not falter. Smoke's ghost-form might be vulnerable to Angel-poisoned machetes, but not to the Volcano Girl's flames. She simply swept her vomit-stream through the corridor and immolated everyone, Legionnaire and superhero, passing the conical stream of fire back and forth and up and down to catch every body and thwart any acrobatics of her foes. Smoke shimmered into smoke, flitting backward unharmed by the flames to reform by her side, while the Legion goons were summarily rendered to smoking ash and bone bits.

It took much longer for her to get the vomiting under control this time, almost five full minutes. It was getting harder and harder to stop throwing up every time she did it; her hourly power-puking fit was coming on fast, and that would spell the end for the warehouse and anything they might hope to recover from it. Smoke stood guard beside her facing the other way down the corridor, one hand holding his sword and the other comfortingly rubbing Neomi's heaving back as the gigantic fireblasts forced up her throat and out her mouth to devastate everything in front of her. Half the personnel area was in burning ruins by the time she finally choked down the flames and swallowed them. Smoke looked at the inferno in front of them, the corridors and offices buried in flaming rubble with their walls and roof collapsed, and shook his head.

"We'll double back the other way," he said mildly. Blowing out clouds of smoke as she panted for breath, Neomi wiped the ash from her lips and nodded, and she turned about and started walking unsteadily back the way she came, her partner's arm around her shoulders supporting her.

Resistance against them seemed to be drying up. Perhaps the Legionnaires were evacuating, perhaps there weren't enough of them left to mount a counterattack. Only one more patrolling team confronted them, and a few enormous blasts of fire from the girl's mouth quickly scattered them.

They soon discovered the computer room of the building, inexplicably lightly-guarded, and swiftly cleared with a few decisive sword slashes and flame blasts. This room was full of stacked bank notes and credit datachips, but the real jackpot was the data drive of the main computer, likely filled with the critical operational details and financial information of Legion operations throughout the city. This was what they had come here for. They took the drive and as much money as they could carry, and Neomi regretfully vomited into the room until the rest was all burned to ashes. They were now carrying hundreds of thousands of dollars in plunder, an almost inconceivable sum of money to the impoverished superheroine, and she tried not to think about it as they moved on.

Only one objective of their operation remained: the production facility itself, which would manufacture the deadly blue pills in bulk.

"The Legion will make their last stand against us there," Smoke predicted. "When the core of the robotics facility is in sight, you can unleash your full power and destroy everything. I just have to make sure that they haven't evac'ed the core by the time we get there."

"What does the core look like?" Neomi asked.

"I want you to see it for yourself. You'll know it when you see it," was his enigmatic reply.

They reached the big double doors leading to the main work area of the building. The doors were locked and chained, and through their plexiglass windows the duo could see that they were heavily barricaded with crates and barrels on the other side. A single tremendous blast of flames from the small girl's mouth exploded through the blockage in an instant, along with much of the walls and roof about it. Such obstacles were useless against the Volcano Girl's terrible power, and she and her sword-bearing companion boldly proceeded through the smoking, gaping hole into the cavernous hangar area of the warehouse.

The hangar was choked with futuristic-looking robotic machinery, conveyers and processors and mechanical contraptions everywhere. But the superheroes' primary objective was visible as soon as they entered. It was the source of all light in the area, emitting a shining pale glow like a window into a cloudless midday sky. And time seemed to slow down, and every other visible detail grew insignificant, as Neomi realized what she was seeing.

In the center of the area, atop a pyramid of robotic construction, was a plexiglass cylinder big enough to hold several people. Several Legionnaires were working frantically to detach it from its crucible, but Neomi barely noticed them. Inside the cylinder was… a *wing*. A great white-feathered wing like that of a human-sized giant dove, glowing brightly enough to illuminate the entire hangar. Chains with barbed hooks cutting cruelly into its flesh held the wing securely in place. And from the stump of the wing that would have connected it to its bearer flowed a slow, continuous dripping of glowing blue liquid: a shimmering, sky-blue liquid of the exact hue of that within the Blue Angel pills.

"But… but… angels aren't real," the girl whispered. Smoke didn't answer her. He didn't have to. The wing shined before them.

She could see now that there were plexiglass tanks of what looked like human blood set in a conveyer system circling the crucible of the wing. Before her eyes, a single droplet of the glowing blue blood fell from the crucible dispenser into a tank of the normal red blood below, and the crimson fluid roiled and paled and begin emitting light as it changed colour, swiftly transmuting to an identical shining blue substance as the catalytic droplet. The tank joined a line of identical tanks on the conveyer bearing them into the convoluted robotic processing system, but the implications were obvious. This was how Blue Angel essence came into being, and its apportioning into gel capsules was just the final step. Its source was there before her eyes: a beautiful white wing cruelly torn from the body of some unknowable aerial being, its sacred blood eternally pouring forth to be perverted into a vile metamorphic drug. It was the stuff of nightmares.

"You've seen enough," Smoke said suddenly, his voice growing harsh. "Volcano Girl. Destroy that abomination. Now."

"Wait! Can't we… save it? Maybe bring it back to its owner?"

"Its owner is dead. They all are. It's up to us to cleanse this perversion of their legacy, Neomi. Do it."

Neomi's stomach was churning madly. The revelation of the source of Blue Angel pills was deeply disturbing and sickening, and it wasn't likely that she could hold the flames down much longer anyway. The plexiglass of the cylinder-prison looked very thick and possibly resistant to her regular flames, so she took a deep breath and retched forcefully at the pyramid, expelling a blazing fireball from her mouth toward the crucible of the wing. An explosive fire-missile to crack the glass first, then she would burn it all away. The projectile streaked through the air and detonated like a rocket grenade… several dozen yards away from the periphery of the robotic pyramid. Astonished and perplexed, the girl projectile-vomited at the crucible again, only to see the missile explode harmlessly a distance from the target once again.

She saw it then: a dark curtain of swirling shadow was between her and the pyramid, difficult to see at first but growing more and more visible by the second, dampening the pure light from the wing. The barrier was tall and wide, completely blocking off half of the warehouse hangar from the duo, and horrid shapes swirled within; deformed faces and bones, teeth and claws, mouths and eyes, monsters and demons, barely glimpsed within the dark. All light in the warehouse was fading fast.

"Oh no. No, no, no," said Smoke, and the fear in his voice chilled Neomi to the bone. "He's not supposed to be here. It's Nemesis."

"Smoke, get us out of here!" Neomi gasped, seizing his arm. "Hurry!"

"It's too late. He's seen us," said her partner, his voice growing oddly calm. "He'll follow us if we ghost-walk now. We have to face him here."

"SMOKE!" a powerful voice boomed through the hangar, deep and smooth and puissant. "It's been too long. How's it hanging, you old fart?"

The man himself had emerged from his dark curtain. Moxxa's ragged long coat billowed impressively as he strode toward them, his living shadows streaming off his back like a royal cape. His great swords and pistols were sheathed, but a palpable aura of menace radiated from him. His blue-glowing eyes shined coldly under the brim of his battered fedora, framed by his long straggly hair and cruel features, yet his voice and attitude conveyed only endless, genial amusement.

"Nemesis." Smoke answered. He stepped forward in a relaxed pose, but he had placed himself between the supervillain and Neomi. "You're looking well. I didn't think I'd see you here, how did you know we were dropping in?"

"Oh I didn't. I was heading out of town, but I stopped by to pay my respects. Just my good luck you decided to come and play here tonight," the dark lord mused. He effortlessly vaulted over a massive conveyer system as he continued toward them. "Now, who's your lovely little girlfriend? Is that little cutie the famous fire-breather who's been giving us so much trouble?"

"Yes she is!" Neomi suddenly called out to him. She stepped forward to stand beside Smoke and assumed her heroic pose, fists on her hips, feet spread apart, chest outthrust and head held high. "I am Volcano Girl, and this is my city. You've made a mistake coming here this night, Finn Moxxa. Shadow is no match for flame, and I will burn you alive if you dare challenge me!"

"Oooh. Feisty!" said the Legion Lord, breaking into a wide toothy smile. "I love it when the young ones show a bit of spirit. Nothing bores me so much as a shy little delicate flower. Such a pretty one too! You've got quite a hottie on your hands, you old dog. And she's literally a spitfire to boot. Tell me, is she this much fun on her knees?"

"Don't you even look at her, *shinigami* scum," Smoke answered in a low, soft voice, and he whipped out his sword in a flash of black steel. Neomi was momentarily nonplussed. She wasn't used to men treating her like this, coming on to her, fighting over her. Even though she despised the dark lord, even though she considered him lower than dirt, she was starting to blush.

"So is it time to dance already?" Nemesis drawled, as he drew out his two long blades with a languid, leisurely grace. "I loved all these little chats with you Smoke. I'm sure gonna miss them."

"As will I. You won't be quite so talkative when you've been parted from your head," said Smoke, and all of a sudden he... was not there.

Neomi just had time to register the faint misty outline of where he used to be. Then there was a mighty clash of steel and she wrenched her gaze toward the Legion enforcer. Her mentor's body still wasn't fully formed, yet his black blade was fully tangible and pressed to the 'X' shape of Moxxa's crossed swords. Somehow the dark lord had anticipated Smoke's surprise attack and parried his lethal ghost-strike with grace and ease. Nemesis casually kicked Smoke away from him, a powerful blow to the gut that sent him flying backward; the superhero somersaulted through the air and landed on his feet in fighting stance. Then the duel began in earnest.

As the clanging of sword against swords rang out, the girl was torn. Should she help her mentor? Or should she assault the crucible of the wing while Nemesis was distracted? The decision came to her quickly: should the wing be spirited away, it could be tracked down another day. But if Smoke was defeated, there wouldn't be another day for him. And besides, he was her superhero partner. Partners took care of each other, that was the hero's way.

Fire exploded from the girl's mouth almost before she came to her decision. She turned the monstrous stream of flames on both of the sparring swordsmen; Smoke shimmered into mist and flitted away unharmed, while Nemesis crossed his swords to make his 'X' shield in front of him and faced the blaze directly. The tremendous force of the blast pushed the enforcer backwards, his booted feet scraping against the floor as he leaned into the shockwave, but the flame itself was sucked into his blades like steam into a vacuum, leaving the towering supervillain unharmed. He abruptly sprang out of the stream, flying through the air toward the fire-spewing young girl; Smoke tackled him from the side, sword scraping against sword as they tumbled to the ground still striking at each other, then Neomi's flame-stream swept over them and they separated and jumped away.

A deadly dance of superhuman combat ensued. Smoke appeared and disappeared, striking at the dark lord from every side, coming at him with spectacular displays of acrobatics and swordsmanship. Neomi vomited out great torrents and bursts of flame, salvoes of explosive fireballs, colossal blasts of white-hot Sunfire, searing globs and geysers of crimson Magmite and green Plasma, and every combination of her stomach's volcanic emissions that she could think of. The enforcer blocked and evaded and absorbed it all, his huge cobalt-blue blades swinging with inhuman speed and grace to defeat every incoming attack. But aside from the occasional kick or shoulder-shove, he rarely counterattacked. Neomi couldn't tell whether Moxxa was being hard-pressed to do anything but react, or whether he was just biding his time and toying with them, and she was growing increasingly worried and scared.

After a time, there was a peculiar moment of stalemate. The sword-sparring and flame-blasting ceased. Neomi was down on one knee, blowing out clouds of billowing white smoke from her scorched mouth as she gasped and panted for breath. Smoke stood a few paces to her side, holding to his implacable fighting stance but breathing heavily and sweating profusely. Nemesis stood before them, making a triangle of the three combatants; he stood with his swords embedded upright in the floor before him, nonchalantly brushing ashes from smouldering spots on his long coat and flicking glowing blue blood droplets from rapidly-closing blade wounds. He seemed poised, relaxed, amused even, and not fatigued in the slightest. Was this his strategy then, to wear them out in a battle of attrition?

"It's been fun, boys and girls," the dark lord drawled. "But the party's almost over. Let's finish this up, shall we?"

"By all means. Surrender and we'll spare you," said Neomi bravely, a lot more bravely than she felt.

"You can't stand against the two of us forever. You'll make a mistake sooner or later, and then you will perish."

"By Jove, what a wildcat you've got there Smoke!" Nemesis answered, smiling broadly. "I can totally understand how you feel about her, old man. It's a shame, really. She's your only real weakness. Your love for her makes you soft. You would be a perfect fighter if not for her. Such a pity. The consummate warrior, brought low for love of a girl."

"You understand nothing," Smoke calmly replied, unfazed, even as Neomi almost fell over with astonishment. "Our bond strengthens us, while you have become complacent in your power. That is why you will fall."

"Sure thing. But not today."

Moxxa reached down and plucked his swords from the ground. Then, suddenly, all light seemed to flee from him and he became a sinister black shadow of himself, the only visible features in the darkness being his coldly glowing blue eyes. A howling wind began to rush through the hangar, and the plentiful light from all the flaming debris began to dim and fade away.

"He's calling on the Black Wind!" Smoke exclaimed. "Look out Neomi!"

Everything was happening so fast, Neomi barely had time to register what was going on. Moxxa's shadowy form seemed to blur and rush toward her with blinding speed. And then Smoke was suddenly before her, shimmering into existence to block the Legion Lord's charge. There was a mighty clash of swords, and the dark lord's strike was arrested midair by her partner's sword, the two long blades crossed in an 'X' shape as Smoke's sword held them back in the middle, like a pair of scissors obstructed by a pencil.

There was a moment where the two swordsmen were standing almost eye to eye, pressed against each other, Smoke's boots scraping backward on the ground as the larger man bore down on him. Nemesis made a low, sinister chuckle that somehow seemed amplified by the screeching wind. Then the two longswords scythed apart, as if the scissors were cutting the pencil in half.

Smoke's black Dao sword was cut cleanly in twain. The warrior froze in place for a brief moment, staring at his bisected sword while the top half clattered to the floor. Then the bottom half fell to the ground as well, and Smoke... faded away. Neomi's mentor was no more.

"*NOOO!*" Neomi screamed, in horror and despair. Her stomach vengefully erupted through her mouth at once, expelling the most forceful torrent of flame it ever had before, a thundering blast that enveloped Nemesis and the majority of the warehouse space instantaneously. She couldn't see anything but the inferno in front of her, couldn't stop crying, couldn't stop vomiting, just couldn't stop. Her emotions were out of control, and so was her power.

A tiny, piercing blue light shone through the cone of flame blasting forth from the small girl's mouth. It slowly moved through the stream toward the origin, steadily pressing forward like a salmon swimming upriver. It was revealed briefly as a Blue Angel pill, held snugly between two shadowy fingers that were absorbing the fire like a sponge, just as it passed between her jaws and was pushed into her mouth. It disintegrated at that point, torn apart by the gushing flames, but that didn't stop some of the vaporized Angel essence from touching her tongue and lips.

The volcanic torrent abruptly stopped. Neomi gagged and retched and sputtered, but no more fire came out of her. The fiery glow in her belly steadily changed to a cold sky-blue. She clutched her stomach and shuddered all over as her blood seemed to turn to ice-water in her veins.

"I have you now," said the shadow before her, as the roiling clouds of flame around it dispersed. And then the shadow itself dispersed to reveal the dark lord Nemesis, whole and unharmed, smiling a broad and feral smile. "At last, the Volcano Girl tastes the power of Heaven. Welcome to the Legion, girl."

Neomi stared at him, still gagging and dry-heaving, hatred burning in her eyes. Never had she hated anything with such cold fury as now. This monster had taken away the one person she cared about most in all the world. She wanted nothing more but to destroy him, almost as much as she wanted Smoke back.

"Oooh, you're angry, aren't you?" the Legion Lord taunted her. He nonchalantly picked up his great swords from where they had fallen, pausing a moment to scratch his back with one of them before sheathing them in their shoulder scabbards. "You go ahead and hate me now. Hate me with everything you've got, it's all good. It will only make the change faster. You'll love it, don't worry. When it's finished, you'll wonder how you ever made do before. You'll be the greatest weapon the Legion ever had, and you're gonna love every second of it."

Neomi opened her mouth, and closed it, and opened it again, struggling to talk. She wanted so badly to be able to talk, to tell this Moxxa how wrong he was, how she would never join him. She felt very strange. Her mind, her emotions, her personality was changing. She could feel it. But there was one thing that wouldn't change, that couldn't change. It was her love for her lost mentor Smoke. As her other memories faded, she remembered how much she loved him, how much she wanted to say to him all the things that would never be said now, how much she wanted him back. And that love made her remember who she was, and that made her remember how much she hated Finn Moxxa for taking her beloved away from her.

The girl's mouth opened, and closed, and opened again. And then all of a sudden, from her open mouth a titanic blast of fire erupted forth, an eldritch fire the same colour as the cold blue light in her belly. The blue flames thundered through the warehouse, and everything they touched was flash-frozen in an instant, covered in a sheen of glassy diamond-hard ice. The burning warehouse suddenly was turned into an icy winterland, and Finn Moxxa was covered in ice up to his shoulders. His dark power could not absorb this attack of withering cold, and the coating of ice quickly crept up to his neck.

"Well. That's unexpected." He sounded only amused, not frightened but filled with endless, genial amusement. Then the blue flame-stream came up over his head, and he was rendered to a statue of ice, right up to the fedora.

Neomi continued uncontrollably vomiting the strange frostfire for a long time, weeping continuously as her blue flames petrified the warehouse before her. She was power-puking as violently as she ever had before, her stomach fully unleashing its volcanic wrath through her small mouth like a tsunami through a pinhole, but only in the form of the mysterious blue Cryoflame. An entire half of the warehouse was frozen before her, the other half in flames behind her. The glowing Angel wing was long gone by now, successfully evacuated by the fleeing Legionnaires while the three superhumans had been fighting, and she could not care any less.

It took a long while, but she eventually managed to stop throwing up the blue frostfire. She staggered and fell to her knees, feeling like she was going to turn to ice herself, but warmth was slowly creeping through her chilled body. The piercing blue glare in her belly gradually returned to its normal fiery orange-yellow glow. She stopped crying and looked down at herself in dull wonderment. She… wasn't turning into a Legionnaire? She had resisted the curse of the Blue Angel blood?

The girl deliberately retched, experimentally, and burning flames immediately spouted up her throat and sprayed out from her mouth. It was just a brief yard-long spout, the smallest discharge of flame her stomach could produce, but it was inalienable proof that her superhuman physiology had returned to normal.

She looked up to see the towering statue of the frozen Legion Lord before her. A rush of hot hatred ran through her, and the fiery light in her belly flared. The dark lord expected that she would have turned to his side, did he?

"You're wrong. You lose."

Neomi took a deep breath and stopped resisting her relentless nausea completely. A gigantic geyser of flame erupted from her wide-open mouth and smashed through the statue of Finn Moxxa, and through the ice-encrusted pyramidal machinery, and through the entire frozen half of the warehouse itself. Everything was smashed apart, the alternation of glacial cold and searing fire shattering it all like glass before a wrecking ball. At its far end the cone of flame was wide enough to immolate a battleship, the most powerful expulsion of flame she could disgorge, nearly eclipsing the geyser of Cryoflame she had just power-puked out, and she swept the fire stream back and forth before her till most of the warehouse was fully consumed by the raging inferno.

As usual, it wasn't hard to let out this magnitude of flame, especially not after the tumult of emotion and battle she had just experienced. It was easy, very easy. The challenge came when it was time to stop vomiting out the flame. That wasn't easy. That was hard, very hard. But it was normal for her, and amidst the torturous discomfort she felt reassured that at least she was herself again.

After a prolonged struggle with her exultant stomach she managed to force the great stream of flames down and swallow it, and when the clouds of fire and smoke dispersed, all she could see before her was a ravaged burning wasteland. There was nothing left for the Legion to recover now. She was done with this place, forever.

Then the girl noticed something. She looked downward, to a few paces in front of her. There she saw two frozen boots, still encased in ice, cut off a foot above the ground. That was all that was left of Finn Moxxa. No… that wasn't right. These were only the icy shells that had covered the boots, like hollow glass sculptures. There were no burned boots or charred flesh within the shells. It was almost as if the remnants of Moxxa had dissolved into nothingness. Dissolved… or faded away into shadow. Neomi felt a renewed chill run through her body. Was Smoke's murderer truly dead? Or had he changed into incorporeal shadow and escaped?

This was just like the comics. Of course he had escaped. The supervillain masterminds always escaped to threaten the superheroes another day. The dark lord was even named after the word for archrival, for an eternal enemy. The Volcano Girl had not seen the last of Nemesis. She was sure of it.

Her eyes fell on something a short distance away on the floor. The two halves of her mentor's black Dao sword laid just a few yards behind the boot-sculptures, surprisingly unharmed by the torrents of frost and flame that had passed just above them. Fresh tears welled up as she slowly plodded over to the fragments, all that was left of the phantasmal man she had loved, the man who just might have been in love with her. She fell to her knees before the sword-halves, weeping silently as she reached out and ran her fingers over the flat of the blades. The prospect of going on without Smoke to guide her, to sustain her, to enrich her, seemed insurmountable.

Grief washed over Neomi in waves, and nausea inexorably followed. Her stomach predictably reacted to her emotion and swelled with pent-up flames, blazing brightly in her belly, and the relentless need to vomit soon overwhelmed her. She just let it happen, turning her head away from the blade halves as the retching started, just allowing the flames to pour from her mouth and the tears to pour down her face. She had never lost someone dear to her before; she had never had someone dear to her before, and the pain of it was near unbearable.

But then a thought occurred to her, a thought that filled her with rising, poisonous hope. Swords could be... repaired. Couldn't they? Mechanics and electricians welded metal together all the time, using focused flame from blowtorches... could she use her own flame to weld Smoke's sword into one piece again? The cut in the blade was a clean cut, perfectly straight, and should fit together like the pieces of a jigsaw... This was no ordinary sword, and she had no skill in working metal, but still...

Still spewing fire, Neomi frantically wiped the tears from her eyes, then she constricted her throat and stomach and narrowed the 'O' orifice of her lips. The flames freely gushing from her mouth lost their billowing conical form and focused into a narrow, intensely hot stream, dwindling in length till it was just a yard long. She carefully picked up the two halves of the black sword, one small hand gripping the handle of the lower half and the other hand carefully holding the cut-off top half by the flat of the blade, minding the razor-sharp edge. And then, as carefully as she possibly could, she gradually brought the two pieces together within her stream of fire.

Clouds of sparks began to fly forth. She turned the blade within the stream so that her flames flowed over one side then the other, trying to keep it perfectly straight and even. She periodically lifted the sword over the stream to inspect the glowing crack: the black metal was unnaturally tough and did not yield easily even to her super-hot fire. At intervals the flame stream stopped so she could snatch a breath between the involuntary retches, and she struggled to keep the process even and steady.

Ever so slowly, the broken blade fused together. Eventually she couldn't see the crack at all, just the glowing strip on the blade. She cautiously passed her fire stream over the damaged part several more times, hoping that the inside of the blade had bonded properly. Then she lowered the sword and turned her face to the side, so she could wrestle with her stomach until she stopped vomiting the flames. It didn't take long to regain control of herself, less than a minute, but she was almost shaking with impatience and anticipation the whole time. Had she done it? Had she successfully repaired the black sword of Zhen Xiaolong?

Neomi looked at the sword. It laid there at her knees, silent and still. The damaged strip in the middle was scarred and pitted, its edge melted away so that there was a gap in the middle of the sword's cutting side. The length was not crooked at least, but it was an ugly repair, even if it was the best she could ever hope to do. She looked around, hoping against hope that a cloud of mist would begin forming before her eyes. When that didn't happen, she sighed and closed her eyes as tears began running down anew. Perhaps it was indeed too much to hope for. If a living human being was cut in half, putting the two halves back together would not bring them back to life. Why would a living sword be any different? She was being a fool, a lovelorn, over-optimistic, heartbroken fool.

But then... she smelled something. Amidst the smoke and char of burning plasticrete and metal, amidst the faint oily scent of vaporized Blue Angel essence and the strange wintery scent of her Cryoflame's ice, she could smell a dry ashen odor that was oddly pleasant. A very familiar odor, a cool ashen body odor that was the only thing that could ease her constant nausea. An odor that was emanating from just behind her.

Without opening her eyes, the young girl jumped up, whirled around, and threw herself into Zhen Xiaolong's arms. His warm strong arms wrapped around her and she snuggled into his embrace, burying her face in the crook of his throat and weeping with a joyousness that almost quelled her nausea outright. She would have kissed him, but she was far too short to reach his face with hers.

"Neomi. You saved me," Smoke whispered, stroking her hair as she sobbed and laughed and quivered in his arms. "You brought me back. I'm alive again. I don't believe it... I don't understand... but I'm alive again. Are we safe? Where is Nemesis?"

Neomi pulled away slightly so she could look up at him. She reached up and fumbled with his ninja mask till his face was fully exposed, and she affectionately placed her small hand on his cheek.

"Nemesis is gone," she said, smiling. "I drove him off, I think. He's not coming back. Smoke… there was something Nemesis said. He said you loved me. Is that true?"

Smoke's grey eyes gazed down into hers for a long moment, then he whispered: "Yes. I love you. I've always loved you. I haven't loved anybody for a very, very long time… but I love you."

"Why didn't you tell me? You idiot!" she growled, but it was a mock-growl that was full of joy. "Smoke, I love you too. I loved you from the day I saw you. We could have been together ages ago, but you had to be all dark and mysterious and snooty… you freaking idiot! Kiss me Zhen! Right now!"

She went up on tiptoes, closed her eyes, turned her face upwards, and puckered up her lips. Smoke hesitated only a moment before his lips gently pressed to hers. It was the most wonderful moment of her life, it was the most delicious feeling she had ever felt. She wrapped her arms around his head and kissed him, repeatedly, for a long time.

At one point, burning debris from the warehouse's collapsing ceiling crashed to the scorched floor nearby. Neither of them noticed.

Eventually they stopped kissing. Neomi looked up at him and giggled, and she wiped the ash from his lips, the ash that had been on her own lips. But her mirth faded as she saw the burgeoning sadness in his eyes.

"Neomi. I can't stay with you for much longer," he said, his voice full of sorrow. "My life force is fading again. I can feel it. I think I'll only be able to take physical form for a few minutes at a time. I need to give you the data drive and all the money I picked up. I should give you my scabbard too, so you can carry…"

The girl abruptly yanked Smoke's head back down to her upturned face and kissed him again. If she only had visitation time with him, she didn't care to waste it on words. Her mentor, soon to be her lover, held her close as his cool white mist rose up all around them, and then they were… somewhere else.

* * *

Transitions

Neomi Eid sat at the edge of the derelict skyscraper's roof, letting her feet dangle over the edge of the abyss. It was close to sunset, and the dim sunlight shined down on her through the clouds. The ruined landscape of inner-city Meridian sprawled below, long shadows looming as the deadly nightlife stirred in readiness.

Neomi wasn't wearing her frumpy black dress anymore. She had a real superheroine's costume now: long boots and long gloves, long flowing cape and mantle, a ninja-style facemask with the lower half of her face and her mouth uncovered, sexy contoured breastplate with a prominent letter "V" incorporated into the wide cleavage, skimpy bikini bottoms that left her round glowing belly fully displayed, all of fireproof materials in fiery red and glossy black. It was entirely too revealing and provocative for a young teenager, and that was exactly how she liked it. Life was too short to waste, her life especially, and she was determined to be as glamorous and sexy as any comic-book heroine in the time she had left.

She reached back and lovingly ran her fingers along the handle of the black Dao sword sheathed over her shoulder. For a moment, a ghostly silhouette of a man formed beside her from the blowing dust and smog, his gentle hand over hers as they grasped the handle together. She had the strength of two superheroes now, with the sword and powers of the great warrior Smoke at her disposal. They were still a team, even if she was the only one visible, and any who would harm her would have them both to reckon with. And when their mission's duties were over for the night, when Smoke could materialize freely without any need to save his life-energy for the exertions of combat, their time together was spent in a dreamy haze of joy and love.

So much had changed since that fateful, frightening moment in her parents' upstairs bathroom, barely a year past. The miserable, self-hating, despondent bulimic that she had been was all but purged from existence now. When she looked down at herself, she saw a body that she liked, in a vocation that she liked, in a life that she liked. She liked herself. That was so alien to her upbringing that it felt strange to think of even now, even though she had forged her new self so many months ago.

Neomi had reconciled with her once-abusive parents. The lavish monthly gifts of cash had certainly eased things between them, plus the simple fact that she didn't live in their house any more. And as she appeared more and more often in the local news, her parents' sullen acceptance of their superhuman daughter had slowly turned to a sort of sullen admiration. Her mother had even come right out and said that she was proud of what Neomi was doing, even if she was a whore for sleeping with "that Asian vigilante". It was a start, and she was quite happy with that.

Nowadays, Neomi lived in a comfortable safehouse in an upscale district of the city, supplied and paid for by the city's secret crimefighter network. Smoke had been a founding member and an active participant in the network, and now she carried on his role and his legacy. She hobnobbed with other superheroes now, even participated in joint operations at times, and she felt valued and welcomed by her new social circle. Her friend Bloodborne, the son of her school's vice-principal, was an especially cherished companion, and she seemed to be growing closer to him and the other heroes every day. She still went to school in the daytime, to the adulation of her adoring fans, but the night was where she exuberantly lived her life now.

Suddenly a strange scent shocked Neomi out of her musing contemplation. It was the oily alien taint of Blue Angel essence, merged with a reeking animal musk like some wild gangrel thing that had never known soap and water. The fiery glow in her belly abruptly changed to a bright cold blue, and she spun around and retched a massive blast of shimmering blue Cryoflame at the monstrous wolf-creature silently sneaking up on her from behind. The giant slavering Hound was flash-frozen in an instant, and it slowly toppled over onto its side like a statue of diamond-hard ice.

As the blue glow in her belly returned to its normal fiery hue, the girl moved over to the ice-encased beast and prodded it with her foot, studying it intently. She had learned something of the biology of the mutated animals the Legion used in their living arsenal, and a brief examination revealed to her that this Hound was much larger, less degenerated and more thoroughly transmogrified than most others of its kin, suggesting it was recently spawned from an extremely pure concentration of Blue Angel essence. Now *that* was interesting. A new Hound, transformed with fresh undiluted Angel essence? Only the dread Legion Lords knew the secret of creating the altered beasts, and for a new one to appear spawned with this purity of Angel blood…?

Could it be that Finn Moxxa was back in town?
A tumult of emotion whirled through her at the thought of her arch-enemy. Hope, and hatred, and anticipation, and excitement, and fear, all rushing through her blood. Her tempestuous stomach reacted eagerly, and burning bile rose in her throat as intense nausea churned in her belly. Nemesis. Oh, she wanted him. She wanted to show him how greatly he had failed, how his actions had made her the heroine that she was today, and then she would freeze him solid and burn him to ash. It was the

height of irony that Moxxa's attempt to induct her into the Legion had bestowed on her the power of cold, a power that the dark lord himself was vulnerable to.

Her nausea was rapidly growing unbearable, but she didn't fear it anymore, nor did she hate it, or resent it, or regret it. It was a natural part of her, a trigger and a gauge of her power, and even though it caused her great suffering she didn't wish it would go away any more. It just was. She accepted that. And as her nausea rose to the erupting point, she accepted it even now.

Clutching her glowing belly, Neomi doubled over as raging flame exploded from her mouth, a gigantic inferno-blast that lit up the dark city below like the dawning of a second sun. She threw up gush after gush of the billowing flames, each prolonged blast larger than the last, turning her face from side to side as she spewed out the flames in all directions for all to see. And after a while, she stood upright and threw her head back as she vomited straight upward into the darkening sky, shooting out a titanic geyser of fire to light up the entire hemisphere exactly like the eruption of an almighty volcano. It was a message, to Finn Moxxa and all of his kind, and to any who would harm the innocent people of Meridian this night.

Beware. The Volcano Girl was coming.

Advent

The great column of fire blasted skyward from the top of the ruined skyscraper, widening at its apex into a roiling cloud of light and fury. The light illuminated the derelict midtown core of the city of Meridian like a second sun dawning in the night. Periodically it would stop for a few seconds, then another blast would erupt forth into the sky, cycling on and on without cease. All in the city and beyond could see the erupting pillar of flame, but it was meant to be seen by two specific pairs of eyes, whose owners had just now finally reached the foot of the decrepit building.

"Here we are and there she be," said the younger of the two men, and he rubbed his hands and cracked his knuckles in nervous anticipation. "Let's get this show on the road! Can you feel her from here?"

"Can't miss her," the other answered. "That's either her, or a very convincing mind-clone. But I'm pretty sure it's her."

"Wait, what?"

"It's nothing, never mind. I'll let her know we're here."

On the roof of the skyscraper, the Volcano Girl stood straight with head thrown back, the mighty torrent of flame spouting from her wide-open mouth up into the sky. Neomi was in her full superheroine garb, complete with sexy breastplate, long boots and gloves, and flowing cape. Her body was straining with effort, her glowing belly heaving with the exertion of vomiting forth such a powerful expulsion of flame for so long without losing control. And her mind was in a turmoil of excitement and emotion, of brimming anticipation and anxiety that set her nausea to soaring and her flames to blazing with thermonuclear intensity. Yet her spirit was oddly at peace, focused on what she was doing and waiting for the signal to desist. So when the signal came in the form of an eerie, ghostly voice on the wind, she was ready for it, and did not startle.

"We're here, Neomi. You can stop now," said the voice.

With effort, she slowly lessened her mighty expulsion of fire until she was able to choke it down and snap her jaws shut. The great cloud of fire above soon faded and left her in nearly pitch-black darkness; she opened her mouth and disgorged a short and narrow jet of flame to see by, and walked over to the edge of the skyscraper's roof. She looked down over the edge and intensified the flow of flames streaming from her mouth: hardly enough to see to the ground, but more than enough to signal the others down below.

"Yes, I can see you. We're on this side of the building," the voice confirmed. Still shooting forth the stream of flames, Neomi reached back to grasp the handle of the black Dao sword over her shoulder. For a moment, the ghostly silhouette of a man formed from the dust and smog all around her, his hand gently holding her small hand over the sword's handle. And then a shimmering cloud of white smoke rose from the floor all around her and she was… somewhere else.

The duo below saw the cloud of mist form before them; even in the pitch blackness, they both could see clearly through the dark. Neomi's flame blade abruptly shined through the mist as the girl herself formed out of nothingness, then the smoke faded and the three superheroes beheld each other.

Before the Volcano Girl stood her two hero-team companions: Bloodborne and Mindbreak.

Bloodborne was a Caucasian boy of the same age as Neomi, clad in ragged flannel pants with a short dark cape hanging from around his neck, bare-chested and bare-foot, slender almost to the point of emaciation. He was covered in strange, livid knife-slash scars, even on his head and face, and on the center of his gaunt chest was a large, bold tattoo of a crimson teardrop upon which was superimposed a stylized silver cross. He had the hollow dark-circled eyes of one who rarely sleeps, and was bald but for a sheen of dark downy hair. He gave Neomi a welcoming smile, a smile that would have been rather handsome if not for the traces of bright-red blood along his teeth, giving him a distinctly vampiric mien.

The third superhuman, Mindbreak, seemed outfitted more like a sinister secret agent rather than a superhero. This recent addition to their team wore a long dark trench coat, dark leather boots and gloves, plain black pants and turtleneck shirt, a black fedora pulled down low over his brow, and a dark scarf wrapped bandit-style around the lower half of his face. Almost all of his skin and features were covered up thus; his age and race were indeterminate. He might have very much resembled the dread Finn Moxxa in his garb, if not for the large heroic emblem on the front of his shirt: a stylized, circled, white letter "M," superimposed over a dark gray brain depiction, with a blue lightning bolt splitting it up the middle.

"Yo Volcano Girl! What'cha got for us? Anything urgent?" said Bloodborne.

The young superheroine swallowed her flame blade; the fiery glow in her belly briefly turned to a hellish red and she turned her head to the side and retched out a fat spout of searing Magmite, which splattered over the sidewalk and sent up a blaze of crimson fire.

With the pitch-darkness so illuminated, she turned to her companions.

"Hi Ben, hi Mord," she greeted them. "It's not urgent exactly. I ran into some Legionnaires that were moving some kind of heavy equipment. They got away, but Smoke tracked them to a subway tunnel. I didn't want to go into a tight space like that alone, so here you are."

"Subway tunnel? The city subway's been dead for ages, I thought all the transit tunnels were filled in," said Bloodborne, raising an eyebrow.

"Oh but they weren't, were they," mused Mindbreak. "Not all of them. This is where it gets interesting, no?"

The Volcano Girl nodded. "The Legionnaires ran into the tunnel, and they blew it up with explosives to keep us from following them. That didn't stop Smoke. When he ghost-walked through, he made it far enough down to hear what sounded like mining machines. Whatever's down there, it's important enough that they would seal the entrance rather than let us get in. The Legion is up to something, and it's happening underground."

"Very interesting indeed," Mindbreak said. "But pointless. If they've sealed the tunnel, what are we supposed to do? Find a shovel?"

Bloodborne broke into a wide smile. "You haven't seen everything she can do. A little cave-in ain't gonna stop our Girl here."

Neomi blushed a little. "Yeah, I'll handle the blockage. But I can't do this alone. You know I'm scared of being in tight spaces."

"I'm scared of being in tight spaces with *you*," said Mindbreak pointedly. "You have to erupt every hour, right? If that happens while we're in a cave, you'll toast us all and probably bring down the roof."

The girl winced. "Yes, that's true. But I just power-puked up in the sky to signal you, so we've got an hour from now to get this done. We'll just have to hurry up and finish it before I power puke again. That's the way it is with me, you have to work with it if you want to be my partner."

"Don't worry dude, we'll get it done in no time," said Bloodborne confidently. "With all our D.P.S. combined, we'll get in there and clean up and get out in a jiffy."

"D.P.S.?" Mindbreak gave him a questioning glance.

"Damage Per Second. It's a video game word," the Volcano Girl explained.

"Stop that. This isn't a game, 'dude'," said Mindbreak sharply to the younger man.

"Says you. This superhero business is the best fun I've had in my life," Bloodborne retorted.

"You know we're not in this for fun, right?"

"Lighten up man," said Bloodborne, glaring. "You gotta enjoy your work or you won't do your best."

"You won't do your best if you don't take your work seriously either." Mindbreak glared back.

"Alright you two, break it u-*uuhh*!!" Neomi abruptly doubled over gushing a fountain of flames from her mouth, as her volatile stomach reacted to her rising unease. Well, that was one way to quell an argument. Her companions smartly stepped apart as the torrent of fire sprayed over the pavement between them, and they moved with haste to stand on either side of her. Smoke materialized at once, the grey-clad warrior comfortably rubbing the girl's back as she threw up gush after gush of blazing flames down the street. He gave a withering glance to the two young men.

"Please don't aggravate her emotions, boys," Smoke said dryly, raising his voice to be heard over the sound of the roaring flames and the Volcano Girl's noisy gagging and retching. "You know that anxiety makes her get sick."

"Sorry," said Bloodborne sheepishly, extending a hand to rub Neomi's heaving back along with Smoke. Mindbreak folded his arms and looked at the warrior.

"Is this really a good idea, master? Your 'prentice is dangerous. She's like an unstable time bomb. Going underground with her could end very badly, it might be better if she stayed behind."

"Mordecai, remember now, I'm not your master anymore, and she's not my apprentice anymore," said Smoke, mildly chiding him. "Neither of you are novices, you're both full superheroes of the city now. And she assembled this team, which makes her team leader. Not me. When she finishes erupting, you should address your concerns to the Volcano Girl."

Mindbreak nodded slowly. Nothing further was said until the girl eventually ceased vomiting the flames. Mindbreak looked to her as she straightened up and wiped her mouth.

"Neomi, I don't think this is a good…" he started to say.

"I heard you. I'm sick, not deaf," she interrupted him. She folded her arms over her glowing belly and regarded him. "We... we all have our problems. That's just a part of being superhuman. Ben could over-exert himself and start bleeding. You could have your hallucinations any time. We just have to accept each other and work together to overcome our flaws. That's part of being a superhero."

"Well said, Boss Girl!" commented Bloodborne. "Yeah, get with the program Mord. We gotta stick together and tackle our problems together."

"The problem is that her problem is worse than ours. Much worse," Mordecai pointed out. "Having to burp up a firebomb any time she feels a little upset is a lot nastier than nosebleeds and hallucinations, and that's on top of the nuclear bomb that blasts out of her mouth every bloody hour. Look, I'm not saying we should abort. I'm just saying it might be better if Volcano Girl stays above ground after she clears the cave-in."

"Yeah and I'm saying you're wrong. We need her," said Ben forcefully. "You and me are pretty good against Legionnaires, but if there's some kind of battle tank down there, or maybe combat robots, or hell, just a really thick metal door, we're stuck. We'll need Neomi to tackle the heavy stuff, and she'll need us to watch her back. Besides, she's the most powerful superhero in the city, maybe in the whole country. You're telling me you don't want that kind of sheer power on our side when we're fighting for our lives?"

"Sure I do. Power like that is handy. What I'm trying to say though, is that she can't control it."

"Hey! That's not fair!" exclaimed Neomi, stung. "I can control my pow-*uuhh*!!"

"Case in point," Mindbreak muttered, flinching away as the Volcano Girl doubled over spewing out great geysers of flames again. He raised his voice to be heard over the raging flames and her noisy retching and vomiting, and said "What if she randomly erupts like this when we're in a bad spot? Like, in an elevator, or trying to sneak around, or in a room full of dynamite?"

"She's actually quite good at holding it down when she's on mission," said Smoke, as he continued rubbing Neomi's heaving back. "She's trained and hardened against throwing up by accident if she's surprised, or scared, or even injured. It's emotional issues and over-excitement that can still set her off without warning. So stop upsetting her and you'll find she's as stable as any other experienced agent in the field. Is that satisfactory?"

Mindbreak seemed to be about to argue further, but he suddenly looked up. His eyes were narrowed as if listening or thinking intently. He looked one way and then the other, seemingly searching for something.

"It will have to do," he said. His voice was low and tense. "We aren't the only ones who saw Neomi's signal. The Legion is closing in, and all this light and noise is drawing them to us. I can hear their thoughts, they're circling around to flank us. We better get moving. Neomi, if you can stop erupting, now would be a good time."

But before he had finished speaking, even as she was throwing up her fiery guts, Neomi was already lurching forward on wobbly legs into an unsteady run. Smoke put an arm around her shoulders to support and guide her as he jogged alongside, and the two young men took up the pace beside them. The Volcano Girl was vomiting so forcefully that her flame stream was ripping up the street in front of her, but this turned to an unexpected blessing as all the trash and debris and broken-up asphalt were vaporized, leaving behind only a smouldering but smooth shallow trench for the team to run through.

Neomi seemed to know where she wanted to go. The team followed as she staggered to a narrow alley between two tall plasticrete embankments, and they watched on with some puzzlement as she deliberately allowed her stomach to erupt out through her mouth with all its volcanic fury. The embankments and the buildings atop them quickly collapsed from the fiery assault, burying the alley in smoking debris. Then, with a supreme effort of will, she slowly choked down the mighty stream of flames until she was able to swallow it completely and snap her jaws shut.

"Okay," she gasped, blowing out billowing clouds of thick white smoke from her mouth as she panted for breath. "Let's get out of sight! Quick!"

"There! Door!" exclaimed Bloodborne, picking out a crucial detail in the darkness with his superior nightvision. "Other side of the street, let's go!"

Moments later, the team were inside a dilapidated apartment building opposite the alley Neomi had just buried. The three men, all of whom could see in the dark, quickly moved to secure the area and make certain they were safe. Their team leader turned to the battered metal door, which hung loosely in its frame and could not be fully closed, and she opened her mouth and shot a narrow stream of flame onto the side of the door, swiftly welding it into the frame and sealing it in place. Now effectively isolated from the outside, the four superhumans reconvened in the center of the building's debris-strewn lobby.

In a cautious whisper, Bloodborne spoke up: "Now what was that all about? Why burn out the alley if we were just gonna hide?"

"It's a decoy," said Mindbreak, a note of admiration coming to his voice. "They'll follow the trench she burned to the alley, and they'll think she brought it down to block them. They'll all be climbing over the alley to follow the false trail, and after they're gone we'll be free to move on behind them. Not bad."

"I do know a few tricks," the small girl said modestly. She blindly held out her arms to Smoke, knowing that his strength would be almost depleted by now, and the grey warrior briefly embraced and kissed his petite lover before dissolving into mist. The remaining three settled down to wait, and Mordecai closed his eyes and listened to the voices only he could hear.

"They fell for it," he said after a few minutes. "They're moving away. Their thoughts are… hungry. And scared. They know who they're hunting, and they've brought some kind of equipment to combat the Volcano Girl's flames. It's a good thing we didn't have to fight them. Well done, Neomi. And Neomi…"

He paused. "I'm sorry for being a jerk. I didn't mean to shake you up, I was just thinking ahead. And I wasn't going to bug out on you anyway, whatever you decided. Are we good?"

Neomi wordlessly reached out a hand and clasped Mordecai's hand in warm acceptance. He might be the newest member of the team and somewhat abrasive at that, but his foresight and perspective were always on point.

In the meantime, Ben had moved to one of the outer windows, all of which were barred and boarded up. He found a tiny crack to peek through, and after a time he said: "I'm pretty sure that's the last of them. The street's clear. Can you pop that door for us, Boss Girl?"

A powerful blast of flames from the girl's mouth immediately smashed through the door, crumpling the melting metal in on itself like tinfoil as it was hurled across the street. Bloodborne was at the doorframe in an instant, checking one way and the other to see if the noise and light had drawn any attention, and after a moment he beckoned his teammates with a wave of his arm. The Volcano Girl started to follow his lead, but Mindbreak abruptly held up a gloved hand. His fedora-topped head turned back away from the doorframe, toward the interior of the ruined building.

"That's not the way. The subway street entrance is this way," he said softly, pointing deeper into the ruins.

"So? You can see the building's collapsed on that side, right?" said Bloodborne impatiently. "Let's get out of here."

"Ben, wait. Did you hear the owl? Look," said Volcano Girl. She took a breath and retched out a sustained burst of fire toward the innards of the apartment building, illuminating the rubble-strewn space. Bloodborne startled a little as he saw what Mindbreak was pointing at: a graffiti image of a large black owl, drawn in ash or charcoal on an intact pillar, with one wing extended toward the deeper dark.

"I swear that thing wasn't there before," said the lad, staring.

"It wasn't. Only I could see it," said Mordecai. "If you're now seeing it, that means things are changing to match what I see. And I see that our feathered friend is pointing the way to a very special door. Can you see it now?"

"That is bloody creepy," Ben said, his gaze turning to the shadowy door looming from the rubble a distance away. "Changing reality to match your hallucinations… that crap's right out of Hush Mountain."

"Hush what?"

"It's a horror video game," explained Neomi, stifling a giggle.

"Didn't I say to stop that?"

"Dude, if it wasn't for video games, I'd be a headcase just like you."

The team moved toward the mysterious door, picking their way through the rubble with Mindbreak leading the way. At the door, he saw that there was no doorknob or handle, or any other visible feature of any kind. He cautiously extended his gloved hand to the surface. Without a sound, the door swung open wide before he touched it.

A sterile-looking white-surfaced corridor laid beyond the shadow door, looking very like a corridor in a medical building or clinic. Cold white light banished the darkness, shining down from bare ceiling strips. Mindbreak hesitantly stepped through. As Bloodborne and the Volcano Girl moved to follow, he murmured: "Keep moving. Don't stop, ever. And whatever you do, don't look into the cell doors. What's in there, you won't be able to un-see."

"You've been here before, haven't you," said the Volcano Girl softly. It wasn't a question. Mindbreak did not reply.

"Why exactly are we taking this detour through nightmare land?" asked the younger man, looking around nervously.

"This should take us straight to the subway. We're moving the same distance in the same direction real-time, just through a different parallel space," said Mordecai abstractly.

"I'll pretend like I understood that and move right along," Ben muttered.

The air was cold around them as the team of superheroes moved through the corridor. The corridor seemed to stretch on before them, seeming much longer than it was supposed to be. Faint disturbing sounds echoed from the side doors, some of which were partially open. After a long while, something gradually started to happen: something like rust or decay began to creep along the walls, floor and ceiling around them, barbed chains that weren't there before hung down from above, large pieces of the surfaces of the walls peeled away like flaps of skin to reveal corroded metal and bloody flesh.

"Keep moving!" Volcano Girl ordered sharply, as her companions hesitated. Bloodborne was flabbergasted by the horrific changes around him, and Mindbreak was clutching his head as if in pain. She impatiently waved an arm to them. "We're almost through! Look, the door's right there!"

The door at the end of the corridor was not being affected by the supernatural decay happening all around them. Neomi started walking very briskly, and fire immediately burst from her mouth as her stomach revolted against the jolts of her quickened pace. She kept going, gripping her belly and rhythmically spewing out big gushes of flame every few steps, but she did not lose control. Her companions were careful to stay at her sides and not in front of her, and the three quickly reached the open door and stepped through. The door slammed shut behind them. She retched flames several more times, then slowly relaxed as she settled down.

"Bathrooms. Why does it always have to be bathrooms," Mordecai growled, looking about himself. The three had emerged from a storage closet door in a large, dimly lit public restroom. The room seemed fairly pristine, but in a state of prolonged disuse.

"So this is the men's room, huh," panted Neomi, as she noticed a row of urinals. "It's a lot cleaner than I thought it would be."

"It doesn't look like a hospital washroom. Are we back in the real world?" said Ben.

"Maybe," said Mindbreak. "I'm hearing voices from far away. Those are probably the minds of real people talking, which would mean we're back in our own world. It's probably not just the voices in my head. Probably."

Bloodborne moved to the exit door, taking point as he usually did. He tried the handle, and said: "Locked. Figured."

"Stand back, I'll take it out," said Volcano Girl, and she took a deep breath.

"No, wait! If we're in the subway complex we don't want to attract Legion aggro right away. Let me open it, I can do it quietly," proposed Bloodborne. Neomi exhaled slowly, blowing out a billowing stream of thick white smoke, while dripping tendrils of solidified gore extruded from the lad's fingertips as he turned to face the door.

"It'll be just as noisy if you tear down the door, you know," said Mindbreak, watching quizzically.

Ben didn't reply, just wrinkled his brow in concentration as his tendrils slid into the key slit and into the doorframe gap near the locking mechanism. After a moment, there was a metallic click from within the door, and he smiled in triumph.

"Open sesame," he cracked. "My blood-snakes are useful for more than just smash'n'grab you know."

"Nice job," Neomi complimented him. "I'm not smelling any Legion taint yet. Can you hear anything out there?"

Bloodborne's hearing was as supernaturally sharp as his vision, which was why he'd been confused when the others had heard the phantasmal owl and he hadn't. He pressed the side of his head to the door and was still for a time. The others held still as well, waiting patiently.

"It's coming from a long way down, but I can hear machines. Metal against metal. Sounds like construction work," he eventually said. "And there's something else... um, a train? Yeah, that sounds like a train engine and train wheels. I think they've got a working subway car down there.

"No Legionnaires?" asked the team leader.

"None outside this door. Unless they're holding their breath."

The Volcano Girl nodded and made a hand motion signaling them to advance. Bloodborne opened the door into a pitch-dark space, and Neomi disgorged a flame blade to see by as they proceeded through. Outside the door, they found themselves at the bottom of an underground flight of stairs. Long shadows loomed from the only source of light, flickering and dancing weirdly from assorted objects and debris. Turnstiles and ticket booths and benches laid before them: they were in the old subway entry terminal. The air was thick with dust, trash and debris littered the floor, and all surfaces were dilapidated and disused. At the far end of the terminal, a tunnel with escalators led deeper down, undoubtedly to the train station itself. Even at this distance, the light from Neomi's blade clearly illuminated the caved-in stone and steel rubble that completely blocked the tunnel.

Neomi spotted a small open stall with stacks of old magazines and newspapers, and she retched a burst of fire onto it that subsumed her flame blade and set all the ancient paper alight, sending up a bright bonfire that clearly illuminated the terminal and nullified the need for the blade. The three young superhumans wordlessly moved to the ticket booths and turnstiles that blocked all access to the tunnel.

The turnstile gates were immovable blocks of rust, barring their passage. In response Bloodborne casually leapt clean over the line of chest-high gates and booths, showing off his superior strength, and landed lightly on his feet on the other side. Mindbreak easily vaulted over one of the gates and joined the younger man. But Volcano Girl hesitated, her everpresent nausea reminding her that any athletic attempt to pass this obstruction would result in explosive consequences.

Instead, she took a deep breath as her stomach's glow turned to a bright pulsating green, and then she doubled over gushing a heavy stream of searing Plasma from her mouth, liberally bathing the turnstile and its gate in molten green goo. The obstacle melted away like an ice sculpture in seconds, leaving only a steaming pool of Plasma and liquefied steel before her. She managed to stop vomiting up the Plasma fairly quickly, then she took another breath as the glow in her belly changed to an icy pale blue, and she retched a wintry blast of freezing Cryoflame all over the molten pool. Then, with a safely frozen surface before her, she stepped through the large melted hole in the line of turnstile gates and fencing, smiling shyly at Mindbreak who was staring goggle-eyed under his hat brim.

"Didn't know she could do that eh?" chuckled Bloodborne. "This volcano can shoot out a lot more than fire and lava. She's pretty hot all right, but she can be pretty cool too."

"I have a few tricks," said the girl modestly.

"Any of your tricks good for a few hundred tons of cave-in?" asked Mindbreak, a cynical tone coming to his voice.

"I think I can handle it," the Volcano Girl answered. She moved to the tunnel and looked down at the rubble filling it up, frowning a bit as she thought it through.

"The problem is how to get through it without more of it collapsing in on us," said Ben, coming up beside her.

"Bigger problem: how is she supposed to get through that much rock before she runs out of fire?" said

Mordecai. Ben snorted with laughter.

"She can't run out, bro. She can spit it out all day long, the trouble is stopping it," the lad explained. "She'll pass out after a while if she can't stop."

"I haven't passed out since I got my cape," said Neomi. "Don't worry about me. Just stay alert. And... stand back."

The Volcano Girl took a deep breath as her belly's fiery glow turned to a piercing, blazing white light. Both of her companions flinched away as a tremendous blast of pure solar fire exploded from her small mouth, the pure white flames driving into the center of the caved-in passage and washing through it like water through sand. A tunnel rapidly formed through the rubble as vapour-clouds of disintegrated matter billowed forth, and the two young men stepped further back as they started to cough. Neomi retched another prolonged blast of Sunflame into the hole, then another, and then she forced the flame back down and swallowed it. When the steam cleared, she could see through the glowing tunnel that a dark space loomed at the bottom: she had successfully burned a way through!

Ben stepped up closer to Neomi and peeked down the tunnel to see the result. He was about to congratulate her but then there was a faint rumble from below. The caved-in debris shifted unsteadily around the glowing passage, and burning fragments flaked off and fell from the roof and walls. The smile faded from Bloodborne's face.

"Uh-oh. That hole don't look stable to me," he said nervously. "I don't think it's safe to…"

But the Volcano Girl wasn't finished yet. Even as he was speaking, the pale glow in her belly had rapidly changed to a hellish crimson-red, and she abruptly doubled over gushing a voluminous geyser-stream of blazing magma into the passage. Ben flinched away again from the heat as she liberally hosed the walls and roof of the tunnel with her Magmite, thoroughly coating the surfaces with a thick layer of the sticky molten goo. Mindbreak stared on in amazement as the powerful stream gushed on and on from her mouth, disgorging quantities of the substance far greater than her small body could possibly contain. When she stopped spewing it out a half-minute later, the walls and roof of the passage were smooth and evened out, though it was difficult to see through the seething flames they were emitting.

Neomi barely took a few seconds to catch her breath as the crimson glow in her belly changed to a pale bright blue, then she doubled over again as a torrent of glimmering blue Cryoflame burst from her mouth. The eldritch fire rushed through the tunnel and instantly doused the residual flames, while the

Magmite itself froze solid and was quickly covered in diamond-hard ice. When she finished spewing out the Cryoflames and straightened up, her companions approached and took a look down.

"Now *that* looks stable to me," said Bloodborne, smiling again. "Looks like we got our way through."

"Not quite," Mindbreak interjected. He extended a foot and tapped the frozen ground at the top of the tunnel. "Good job on the tunnel Neomi, but that floor looks pretty glassy. We might have a one-way slide going down here."

"Maybe," Volcano Girl replied, looking down at her work. "My ice takes the same texture as the stuff underneath, but let's not take chances. I better burn us some steps down."

"That's gonna take too long," said Ben. "We don't got much time before you have to power-puke again. I got a better idea."

He paused in concentration for a moment. Blood began to seep from the scars around his bare feet and ankles, visibly darkening and hardening into downward-pointing spikes from his soles. When he was finished, he was effectively equipped with grotesque blood-crampons for climbing.

"I'll carry you," he offered to the team leader, holding out his arms to her. "That way you won't get too sick on the way down. Mord can slide though, this ride is for ladies only."

"Thanks," said Mindbreak dryly. The Volcano Girl thought it over for a moment, then she hesitantly went over to Bloodborne and allowed him to pick her up like a child.

"How romantic," snarked their dark-clad companion. "Well you two lovebirds have all the firepower, so you should go first. I'll bring up the rear."

"Not a good idea," said Neomi, grimacing with discomfort as Ben took a step. "Any kind of climbing makes me really sick. I'm going to bring up even if Ben carries me, better that I shoot it out behind us rather than hit the tunnel in front of us. That means you have to go first Mord."

"Sure hope you don't bring down the roof on us," said Bloodborne worriedly. With effort, she smiled, and replied: "My ice is very hard. It'll hold out long enough, don't worry."

"Okay Boss, I'll take point," Mindbreak shrugged. "If there's any trouble at the bottom, I'll keep 'em busy till you get there. Let's roll."

Squatting down before the frozen tunnel entrance, Mord took a hop forward as if to kick off a snow sled. Into the hole he slid, but not very far or fast. It was hardly the slippery ice slide he was expecting; the ice underfoot was actually quite rough and gritty. He hopped down again and slid further down, and one more hop-slide got him to the bottom.

"I made it. There's nobody here, not yet anyway. Come on down," said his ghostly thought-voice to his teammates.

Bloodborne steeled himself and stepped into the tunnel. His footsteps were soft and steady as a cat's, yet he didn't make two paces before the Volcano Girl's stomach revolted and she spewed a heavy gush of flame over his shoulder and backward up the tunnel. He winced and froze in place; the girl in his arms gagged and retched up several more big spouts of fire, and then she got herself under control.

"Keep going," she whispered to him. "Don't stop unless I start puking really hard. If that happens, run."

Ben nodded gingerly and proceeded onward. Neomi retched flames over his shoulder every few steps, forcing him to move even more slowly for fear of aggravating her nausea further. But despite his best efforts, the blazing blasts gushing from the girl's mouth were getting bigger and hotter with every retch. The tunnel walls began to sweat; rivulets of melt-water began flowing down around his feet. Then there was an ominous rumble from the tunnel roof. He froze in place, his heart pounding. She retched fire over his shoulder one more time, then she seemed to catch her breath and regain control.

"You okay now?" Ben asked.

"Yeah, I'm okay," she answered cautiously. She rubbed her fiercely-glowing belly and took a breath. "I'm okay. You can start moving again, I'm oka-*uuhh*!!"

Her body convulsed suddenly as the fire exploded from her mouth again, this time a giant roaring geyser that thundered up the tunnel behind them and did not stop coming out of her. The back end of the passage shattered immediately, and chunks of ice and rock rained down around them as the tunnel began to collapse. Bloodborne yelped and leapt forward, bounding downward in long powerful strides, nimbly dodging around the falling rocks and the rolling debris underfoot while the Volcano Girl continued violently erupting over his shoulder.

He was out of the tunnel almost in an instant, and very well that he did, for the opening crumbled in scant seconds behind him. Neomi went on vomiting fire over his shoulder, struggling desperately to stop as the gigantic prolonged blasts forced up her throat and out her mouth into the collapsing tunnel. The passage actually persisted for the duration, the falling debris partially vaporizing from the intense heat as it was all blown up and out of the tunnel, inadvertently providing an escape vent for the forceful flames.

"This is what I was afraid of," said Mindbreak to the lad, raising his voice to be heard over the roaring flames. "Don't say I didn't warn you."

Ben glared at him, while he hugged his petite team leader in his arms and rubbed her back. The swirling dust and smoke around them began to coalesce into the shape of a man; Smoke quickly assumed human form beside the two teenagers, speaking softly and comfortingly to the girl as he massaged her heaving shoulders. Neomi's stomach started to settle down immediately. She managed to stop vomiting in a matter of minutes, which was quite quick for her, but an agonizingly long time to her teammates. The tunnel collapsed fully with a deafening crash, and the four hurriedly moved back as the wall of rubble shifted and advanced several paces.

Thick white smoke was billowing from her mouth as she panted for breath, but at her gesture Ben carefully set her down. She wiped the ash from her lips and turned to face her team.

"Sorry guys," said the Volcano Girl. "I guess I ran right into the part about 'us having problems'. Let's just assess…"

"We've got another problem now," Mindbreak interrupted her, scowling. "You just smashed our only way out. When things get dicey it's going to be a big problem."

"She can get us out of here the same way she got us in," Bloodborne growled. "Stop hassling her, you."

"Situational awareness, people," said Smoke firmly before the dark-clad superhuman's inevitable retort. "We're in Legion territory now. You don't have time to argue."

"Smoke's right. Assess this zone now," Volcano Girl ordered. "I can't see a damn thing. Where are we?"

"It's a connecting hub," said Bloodborne, looking around. "More tunnels lead off to the subway platforms and the central trainyard. It's set up like a big lounge, lots of benches and stuff. Nobody's home."

Neomi nodded, and the fiery glow in her belly turned deep red. She bent forward and retched a spout of Magmite onto the ground, and crimson flame ignited and illuminated the area so she could see. The lounge-hub's tunnels were mostly caved in, she realized, but the large passage to the trainyard was conspicuously open and clear of debris.

"Hear that? Heavy machines down that way," said Mindbreak, pointing to the trainyard tunnel. "And I can hear voices from there too… wait a minute. Some voices coming this way. We're gonna have company!"

"Ambush positions!" ordered Neomi in a sharp whisper. "We'll have to take them out fast before they radio for help. Flank that tunnel!"

The superheroes swiftly moved into position. Bloodborne and Mindbreak took their places behind either corner of the tunnel. Smoke actually leapt forward and ran up the wall above the top of the tunnel opening, grabbing a roof strut and swiveling to hang upside down like a bat, ready to drop down on unsuspecting prey. The Volcano Girl moved as quickly as she could to hide behind one of the facing benches, then she retched a burst of Cryoflame on her Magmite flare to put it out, and she drew her cape around her body to cover up her glowing belly. And so, the team settled down to wait. They did not have to wait long.

There was no problem seeing the squad of Legionnaires in the dark; their eerie blue-glowing eyes and arteries gave them away, especially since many of them preferred to go shirtless. They were neither inexperienced nor stupid: having seen from the tunnel that the light that had drawn them had gone out at their approach, they were suspicious and cautious. They advanced slowly, weapons at the ready, till they were at the threshold of the hub space. And then, abruptly, the superheroes sprang into action.

Mindbreak struck first. Stepping out of hiding, the sinister hero went down on one knee and pressed his fingers to his temples as if in pain. Whatever it was that he was experiencing, the Legion gangers were subject to it as well; some fell to their knees clutching their heads, some shrieked and swung or discharged their weapons at enemies that weren't there, some simply froze in place. Many were thus incapacitated, but some were not, and these ones brandished their weapons and charged forth at the only threat they could see.

Bloodborne and Smoke sprang into action. The lad targeted the two conscious Legionnaires with firearms; they only got off a couple of shots before his blood-whip tentacles lashed out and ensnared them, yanking them off their feet towards the young man. Smoke opened fire with his custom autopistol, raining bullets down on the three blade-wielding Legionnaires that charged out of the tunnel towards Mindbreak. All three were hit, one crumpling motionless to the ground, the other two staggering but continuing to press on.

Then the Volcano Girl stood up. A great torrent of fire from the girl's mouth thundered into the trainyard tunnel and vaporized all the stunned Legionnaires in an instant. She turned the fiery stream toward the two Legion bladesmen charging toward Mindbreak, but both managed to jump high in the air and evade her.

Smoke drew his black Dao sword and leapt from his roost, tackling one of the airborne Legionnaires to the ground. The two wrestled with each other as they fell, striking and grappling as they rolled over the floor. The other bladesman reached his target successfully, and Mindbreak just barely managed to turn his body away from the blow to avoid being impaled by the Legionnaire's knife.

Frenetic melee combat ensued, and Volcano Girl was powerless to intervene for fear of burning her teammates. Smoke decapitated his enemy in an instant and rushed to Mindbreak's aid; the dark-clad superhero wrestled feebly with the much larger and stronger Legionnaire, but he eventually managed to whisper a word into the bladesman's ear and his foe froze trembling in place, easy prey for Smoke's lunging sword. Bloodborne was smaller than his two adversaries but just as fast and strong, and he flailed at them with a nightmarish blur of thrashing tentacles and erupting spikes, at one point extruding a plethora of spines like a porcupine to skewer the Legionnaire grappling him from behind. It was all over in a matter of seconds.

There was a moment of silence, save for their heavy breathing. The superheroes were all still for a moment, waiting to see if any of the fallen would rise anew, or if new foes would appear. Light blazed from wall fixtures and furniture set alight by Neomi's flames, and nothing moved. For the moment, it seemed that the superheroes had prevailed.

"Area secure. Good luck heroes," said Smoke, and he dissolved into mist, using the last of his strength to levitate his black sword into Neomi's shoulder scabbard. His ghostly hand briefly twined its fingers with Neomi's as she affectionately grasped the handle, then the veteran warrior was gone.

"Everybody okay? Ben, you look awful," said the Volcano Girl worriedly. Bloodborne was covered in gore, mostly his own. He had been shot and stabbed repeatedly by his enemies, and his own blood-weapons had gouged gaping wounds where they had extruded from his body. He stood still in concentration for a moment, and all the crimson tentacles and spines liquified to normal blood and seeped back into his wounds, which rapidly closed up and healed away. When he had finished absorbing all the blood around him and regenerating his injuries, the lad looked almost as though he had come through the battle unscathed.

"This lot was meaner than most," he commented, prodding one of the deformed corpses with his bare foot. "They're not running this place with the usual trash mobs. These ones were goons. Not quite soloes. But definitely goons."

"Goons? Soloes? What?" came from Mindbreak, who was slowly getting to his feet.

"He's saying these guys were veterans, not ordinary grunts. Mord, did you get hurt?" asked Volcano Girl.
"Just a scratch," the dark-clad superhuman said, somewhat hoarsely. He flicked blood droplets off his lapel: red human blood, not blue-glowing Legion blood.

"Baloney," snapped Ben. "You're bleeding. I can sense it. Hold still, let me take care of it."

"You're using your powers too much," Mindbreak protested as Bloodborne rushed up to him. "You're going to wear yourself out!"

"Shut up and let him heal you," ordered Volcano Girl. "That's not negotiable. How bad is it, Ben?"

"No worries, I got this," the lad replied. He passed his hand slowly over the rent in Mord's shirt, and the gaping wound underneath visibly closed and faded. "There we go, good as new. And don't worry about me, I got plenty of juice left."

"Okay. Let's get going before they notice their missing team," said Neomi, and the superhumans collected themselves and moved to the train yard tunnel where the Legionnaires had come from.

A minute later, the heroes stood before a landing of sorts. Here, there was light: glowing ceiling strips illuminated a sizeable room with a stairway access door, a very large cargo elevator, and several smaller personnel elevators, all marked with "Employees Only" signs. There was no sign of the Legion. The landing had the worn look of a well-used and ill-maintained thoroughfare.

"They've got the power system up," noted Ben. "Those elevators are working. Crap, we have to go down. No other way to go."

Mord had gone up to the stairway door and opened it slightly to peek through. "Staircase is collapsed," he reported. "Not a problem for the Legion to climb and jump, but we're out of luck. It's elevators or nothing."

"Can't you use your freaky reality-changing powers to repair the staircase?" asked Ben.

"It doesn't work like that. I think the ability activates from subconscious urges, but even I don't know for sure. Basically, it has to happen by itself."

"Great," muttered Neomi. "I hate elevators. I don't suppose we can take the big one?"

"No, it needs a keycard," said Ben, spotting the card reader at the side of the massive doors. "The personnel lifts ain't locked though. Guess we got no choice."

"Alright then," she said, and took a deep breath. "Ben, hit the button."

Tapping the call button, Bloodborne reflexively took up an ambush position pressed up to the wall beside the bank of elevator doors. Mindbreak and Volcano Girl did the same on the other side. After a long moment, two of the doors slid open. No one stepped out.

The heroes peered in. One of the doors had opened to reveal a yawning empty elevator shaft, which was decidedly not encouraging. The other door had a proper elevator car waiting inside, but the car itself was coated with rust and filth, which was not very encouraging either.

The three looked at each other. A wordless moment passed between them. Ben shrugged. With Smoke out of commission, their only choices were to enter the dilapidated elevator with a nervous and claustrophobic Volcano Girl, try to climb down the empty elevator shaft or the collapsed staircase while braving the Volcano Girl's motion sickness, or concede failure and go back. None of these options were particularly appealing. The team slowly boarded the only elevator.

Flickering light from the one working ceiling strip illuminated the car. The metal surfaces of the walls, floor and roof were all bare and discoloured with rust. There were only three buttons on the elevator's interior panel. One button had an upward-pointing arrow beside it, the next button below it had a downward-pointing arrow. The last had an alarm bell stencil, but that button was broken with bare wires sticking out. There was a certain grim symbolism in that, but no one was in the mood to comment.

"Hey. There's my owl," said Mindbreak softly. The others looked where he was pointing, and saw. The dark owl was rendered on the side wall, one wing unfurled and pointed downward. "He's pointing at the floor. Huh."

"I can smell oily air coming from the floor. There's a little breeze. Must be a crack," said Volcano Girl.

"We better watch our step."

"Not a crack, a hatch!" said Bloodborne excitedly. He dropped to one knee and scrabbled at the rusty floor. Bloody claws formed from his fingertips and he tore out flakes of rust until he found a ring-handle. One mighty yank pulled the trapdoor hatch right out of its frame, leaving a dark square hole in one corner of the car.

"Now we got a vent in case Neomi needs to puke on the way down," the lad said in triumph. "Let's do this!"

"Wait, there's probably a roof hatch too," mused Mindbreak. "Shouldn't we have her use that? What with heat rising and all."

"Yeah, and that'll melt the winch cables. Good call buddy," said Ben sarcastically. "Okay Boss Girl, you ready?"

"Ready as I'll ever be," she replied, her voice faint and resigned. She took a deep breath, rubbed her brightly-glowing belly, and closed her eyes. "Hit the button."

Bloodborne hit the button. The elevator promptly lurched. Neomi immediately fell to her knees gushing a fountain of flames from her mouth. But she had the presence of mind to aim the blast downward into the hatch opening, saving herself and her companions from a sudden fiery demise. She spewed down into the opening several more times, then she seemed to regain control of herself as the lift's descent became more even and steady. She had grown strong enough to resist this amount of motion normally, but she was so anxious and keyed up that the slightest provocation was enough to set off her roiling stomach.

"I'm okay," she gasped, hugging her belly and gasping for breath. "I'm okay. Just a little nervous. I'm oka-*uuhh*!!"

The elevator lurched again. The Volcano Girl violently erupted into the hatch opening again, spouting blast after blast of roaring fire down the hole. Seething heat flooded through the car. Bloodborne squatted beside her and rubbed her heaving shoulders and back, while Mindbreak stepped back nervously as the edges of the hatch started to melt. Neomi managed to choke down the flames after a few seconds, but the elevator kept periodically lurching, sending her into fits of convulsive fiery vomiting every time. Her anxiety at being confined in such a tight space was intense, and correspondingly, so was the power of the flames exploding forth from her mouth.

It was a long ride down. The floor hatch opening grew wider and wider as the periphery melted away under the Volcano Girl's fiery assault. She was panicky and almost frantic with fear, and that made her flames even hotter, which cycled to make her ever more frightened. After a while, the floor started to sag alarmingly. The backflow of heat was turning the elevator interior into an oven, and the two men sweated profusely as their clothes started to smoke and smoulder. The situation seemed very grim.

"Calm yourself, Neomi," Smoke had once said to her when her stomach was out of control. Even as she was supremely distracted by this excruciating ordeal, somehow she managed to remember his calming words. "You're not a novice any more. Your training is complete, you're an experienced superhero now. You can control it. You know you can."

Her mentor wasn't here. His power exhausted, he was dormant within his sword. But as Neomi drew on her experience and her training to control herself, the presence of Smoke was so pervasive in her mind that she could smell his soothing ashen scent. Her stomach started to calm down. She remembered she was not afraid of her power anymore. The force of the convulsions wracking her body began to lessen. The power and intensity of the fireblasts exploding out of her began to diminish, till she was able to completely swallow down the flow of flames and snap her jaws shut.

"There, I'm finished," she said to her companions. The elevator lurched again, forcing her to retch flame into the hole one last time, but she didn't erupt again, and the continued lurching did not faze her. "Good grief, this machine is like a bucking bronco. I don't know how you guys can stand it."

"Yeah, I'm feeling a little funny myself," laughed Bloodborne, suffused with relief. "Let's just hope this thing makes it all the way!"

"Don't jinx it," said Mindbreak coolly. He wiped the sweat off his brow with a gloved hand, and took a peek down the melted hole. "There's the bottom of the shaft coming up. Looks like we're almost done."

The elevator finally slowed and came to a halt. The heroes hid behind the extruding walls on either side of the entry as the doors slid open. They peeked around the corner, Neomi ducking under Mord's tall frame to do so, and beheld the panorama before them.

A vast cavern laid before them. Dozens of railroad tracks ran across the smooth rock floor, and hundreds of dilapidated train cars laid still and unmoving upon them. Dim light shined down from strip lighting mounted on a catwalk system high above. Asphalt roads ran along and across the tracks in places, and rows of buildings and large cargo containers were periodically arrayed beside the track lines. There were a number of cargo cranes, some portable. And numerous industrial utility vehicles and machines were on the roads and interspersed parking lots, mostly rusted and disused.

But not all of the railyard was in disrepair and dereliction. There was movement. Some of the utility vehicles were on the move, their blazing headlamps illuminating long swaths of the darkened yard. The boom of a cargo crane raised up and slowly swung about, apparently lifting a decrepit train car off its tracks and moving it elsewhere. One building near the center of the yard was larger than the others; rows of blocky electrical batteries and transformers were arrayed around it, and flickering arcs of violet hued lightning-light flashed between the equipment and within the building's windows.

Rangy long-limbed figures loped through the yard, their bodies glowing faintly blue in the dim light. Many appeared to be working, carrying equipment and supplies about, lifting and clearing the rusted debris with superhuman strength, or operating various machines. Others were moving in teams, traversing the grounds in obvious patrol rounds, some accompanied by huge dark wolf-shapes with blazing blue-white eyes. Although large areas of the trainyard were dark and still, dozens if not hundreds of these figures occupied the central zone and some of the regions surrounding it.

And some of them were heading this way.

"Get behind that thing! Quick!" Volcano Girl whispered harshly, pointing toward a large piece of anomalous machinery nearby. "Mindbreak, cover us!"

"I'm on it," said the dark-clad superhuman. Once the three were crouching behind the bank of machinery, Mindbreak pressed his fingers to his temples, concentrating intently. "Almost there… almost all of them… there. All they see is shadow. Nobody make a sound now."

The heroes held still and silent as the team of blue-glowing gangers loped past, none of them so much as glancing their way. The Legionnaires halted at the elevator when its doors opened and they saw the heat damage to its flooring. There was a moment of tense discussion among them, and Bloodborne leaned a little closer as he listened in. The altered criminals chose to forego the elevator and moved instead to the door to the stairwell, and there were distant sounds of clanging and scraping as they began climbing and leaping up the collapsed stairway shaft. Finally, the last of them went through the door, and they were gone.

"Yeah, they're suspicious all right," reported Bloodborne. "They're gonna come running when they find the bodies upstairs."

In response, Neomi wordlessly opened her mouth and expelled a narrow stream of fire at the stairwell door, training the intense flame along the seams of the door and welding it into its frame. She did the same to each of the elevator doors, sealing off all access to the landing exit.

"Nice work, but that won't hold them for long," Mindbreak murmured. "We better get going."

"Where to? This is a bloody big trainyard," said Bloodborne in some consternation. "How are we going to put all this out of action?"

"There," the Volcano Girl answered, pointing. She was indicating the central building, the one with electrical equipment arrayed in its yard and lightning arcing behind its windows. "That must be where they're getting all their power. Subway cars run off electricity. If we shut down the power, we shut down their operation."

"Wait a minute," said Mindbreak. "I'm no engineer, but I do know that power doesn't come out of thin air. Where's that little plant getting the power to run this whole place? The electrical grid in this area has been down for years, so they're not leeching off the city."

"So? Why does it matter?" asked a somewhat perplexed Bloodborne. "Let's burn the thing down and be done with it."

"It matters because of what might happen after we burn it," said Mindbreak. "It's obviously not hydro, solar or wind based. That means it's either a fossil fuel like petrol or coal, which could set off a big fire with lots of choking smoke, or it's…"

"Nuclear." Volcano Girl finished for him, her voice almost a whisper.

"So? So what?" asked Bloodborne, eyebrows furrowed.

"So if that's a micro-nuclear plant and we just torch the thing willy-nilly, we could set off a full meltdown. And that means giant thermonuclear explosion and… adios muchachos." Mindbreak finished grimly.

"Oh great. Wonderful. S%&t." Bloodborne growled. "There ain't no smokestacks on that plant, so it sure as hell ain't coal or petrol. What are we supposed to do with a bloody nuclear power plant? What do we do now?"

"It's too small to be a full nuclear facility with a reactor," said Volcano Girl. "It must be running off a fusion cell."

"Bingo," Mindbreak exclaimed. "It can't be anything else. It has to be using a micro-fusion cell, and those are man-portable. Anybody up for a heist?"

"Great train robbery, huh. Well it beats nuking all our asses, so I'm in," said Bloodborne, cracking his knuckles as he prepared himself.

"Let's do it then. And quickly," said Volcano Girl. "We've got half an hour at most before my next power-puke, and I'd rather be out of here before then."

The three young heroes tentatively stepped away from the safety of their cover and moved into the dark trainyard, with Bloodborne and Volcano Girl leading and Mindbreak just behind. The huge dark forms of the derelict rail cars loomed around them like walls in a maze. Their footing was treacherous; aside from the rail tracks and ties themselves, the ground was heavily littered with rusted metal parts and debris. Mindbreak and Bloodborne were managing to pick their way through the trash with their nightvison, but Volcano Girl wasn't so lucky. She could only cling to Bloodborne's arm, lurching drunkenly when her footing was obstructed, and try to make do as best she could.

Proceeding down a narrow alleyway between train cars, Neomi abruptly tripped over something in the dark, and the volatile fire in her stomach immediately erupted out through her mouth as she stumbled and nearly fell. As she regained her footing, she retched again before she could stop herself, spewing out an even bigger fireblast into the darkness and lighting up the whole alley. Everyone froze in place, still and silent, but the damage had been done.

"They're coming. We have to hide," said Mindbreak's noiseless ghost-voice to his companions.

Thinking quickly, Bloodborne grasped the rusted handle of the adjacent train car's side-door, straining mightily as he slowly forced the massive sliding door open. The car held only a few filthy wooden crates, but the interior walls were liberally splashed with something looking uncomfortably like dried blood. He vaulted into the car at once and reached down to help the team leader aboard; Volcano Girl retched flame again as she struggled to climb in, but she managed to keep control and only let out a small burst that splashed briefly against the far wall. Mindbreak quickly scrambled in behind her.

"Leave it open! Don't have time!" the sinister hero cautioned telepathically as Bloodborne started to force the door shut. *"I'll hide us from their eyes!"*

Once inside, the trio huddled at the far end of the interior of the car. Neomi pressed her hand to her mouth and struggled not to gag at the faint rancid smell of the dried gore, and Ben put his arm around her narrow shoulders in reassurance. The sound of harsh raised voices came in from outside. Mordecai touched his fingertips to his brow and closed his eyes in concentration. There was movement outside, rapid footsteps, debris tossed aside.

"Scorch marks. The bitch was here," snarled a distorted, menacing voice. "I told you the cave-in wouldn't hold her off."

"Shut the f*&k up! These scorches are still smoking!" another distorted voice snapped. "She's close. Search everywhere, under the cars, in the cars, everywhere! And you, Skull! Go tell the Tin Men to get ready!"

The sounds of further commotion came from outside the car, some footsteps rapidly receding, others pacing around close by. Then there was a flurry of movement, and two tall rangy blue-veined Legionnaires leapt into the train car. The heroes all froze, still as statues, as their foes scanned the interior. One of the altered gangers turned his glowing eyes to look directly into their corner of the car, and Neomi's breath caught in her throat. But his gaze passed them by, and he went on searching elsewhere. The other Legionnaire had opened the opposite car door, and it looked like they were about to move on.

Just then, the Volcano Girl felt a warm wet droplet on her arm, and she smelled fresh blood. More droplets followed, and she looked at Bloodborne in alarm. He was bleeding profusely from his nose and weeping tears of blood, and he startled in surprise at the sight of his own gore. Ben's haemophilia had chosen the worse possible time to express itself. He wiped frantically at his face, but it was too late.

The nearby Legionnaire who had just looked their way stopped in his tracks, and his blue-glowing gaze returned to the heroes' hiding spot. He drew in a breath, sniffing the air.

"Hold up. I smell blood. Fresh blood." his distorted voice growled. "They're close. They're very *very* close."

The Legionnaire's voice rose to a roar. "Spike, get your boys in here! Check those crates, now!"

Dripping claws extruded from Ben's fingers, and Neomi's glowing belly flared with nausea as the two teenaged heroes instinctively prepared for battle. But Mord reacted very differently. He abruptly sat down on the floor and closed his eyes as he leaned back against the wall, as if to take a little nap. Ben and Neomi stared at him in surprise. But before either of them had a chance to say or do anything, another roar came from outside.

"F*&k that! We got one of them! Get out here!"

The two Legionnaires looked at each other and then rushed out of the car. In some confusion, Neomi checked on Mordecai's prone form while Ben struggled to get his bleeding under control. Mord seemed uninjured but unconscious. Then further shouting from outside drew Neomi's attention, and she cautiously sneaked to the side of the open door to peek out.

Outside the train car, the Legionnaires had dragged a dark-cloaked form out of the neighbouring car and thrown it to the ground in the midst of them. It was difficult to Neomi to make out details in the near dark, but she could see that the figure was a human-sized male wearing a black fedora. As the figure was pulled up to his knees, it was revealed that he had on a turtlencck and a scarf under a long trench coat. It looked, in fact, very much like Mordecai. Neomi looked back at Mord's prone form in the corner of the car, and then turned to look at the kneeling duplicate of Mord on the outside, and she shook her head in befuddlement.

The Legionnaires dashed the fedora from the figure's head, revealing Mordecai's haggard features and straggly black hair. They began brutally interrogating him, punctuating each demand for the location of "the bitch" with vicious punches and kicks. Faint grunts and gasps of pain drew Neomi's attention back to the other Mordecai. His head was rocking back and snapping side to side with each punch to the duplicate's face, his body convulsing with every kick to the other's gut and groin. Then, she finally understood.

Neomi looked to Ben, who had by now reabsorbed all of his leaked blood and was looking healthy and ready for action.

"Ben, grab Mord, quick!" she ordered in a harsh whisper. "He's made some kind of clone of himself, but it's not gonna last much longer! Let's get out of here!"

The lad was quick to obey, swiftly hoisting the older superhuman's body over his shoulder in a fireman's carry. He jumped out the opposite side-door of the train car and was safely gone in seconds. Neomi thew caution to the wind and clambered out the door in pursuit with a rapid scramble of movement. Her aggrieved stomach promptly gushed fire out through her mouth from the shock of the sudden motion, but the young heroine steeled herself and managed to let out only a brief yard-long spout that drew no attention from the distracted Legionnaires on the other side of the car. And with that she was off and away, moving through the dark as quickly as she dared, following the body-scents of her companions.

Neomi soon caught up with Ben, who had found shelter in an unused storage shed. She closed the sliding door behind her and retched a spout of blazing Magmite onto the floor to light up the pitch darkness. Mordecai had regained consciousness by now and was seated on a blocky piece of mysterious rusty equipment, seemingly to catch his breath. He looked even more haggard than usual and seemed to be in pain, nursing unseen injuries under his clothes. "He's taken a bruising, but he'll be okay," said Ben when their team leader looked to him. "Looks like he suffered everything that they did to his decoy, just not as bad."

"I'll be alright," Mord interjected in a hoarse voice. "My wounds are psychosomatic, they will fade soon enough. But we need to keep moving. My mind-clone has dissipated, that's how I'm talking to you now. That means the Legionnaires have lost their prisoner and will be hunting for us again."

"Well at least we've gotten close to the power station now," said Neomi. Even with the door closed, the piercing light of the station's electrical flares intermittently shined through the cracks in the doorframe, and the deep vibrating hum of the generators could be felt through the ground. "We don't have much left to go. You boys ready?"

"Ready. Sure wish I could have seen their faces when Mord's clone vanished into thin air," Ben smirked. "Let's roll."

The trainyard's power plant was just minutes away, even at Neomi's slow pace. The violet lightning arcs surging between the rows of transformer towers were giving off plentiful light, and the crackle of electricity and the deep hum of generator machinery masked any noise from their approach. The acrid smell of ozone was heavy in the air, and the girl struggled not to gag as they drew closer.

The young heroes stopped at the perimeter of the power plant compound, which was surrounded by a tall wire-fence. They saw that there were two massive gates leading into the compound, one at the front and one in the rear. A relatively pristine subway engine was just inside the rear gate, and there were no Legionnaires in sight.

"There's our way out," murmured Volcano Girl, pointing to the engine car. "That thing looks fully functional. We just have to find the fusion cell now. Guys, what's our opposition?"

"I sense two minds in the top floor of the building," reported Mindbreak. "They're… afraid. Afraid of all the lightning. I think they barely know enough to keep this place running. No other Legionnaires in the area. They're relying on the electrified fence and the thick walls of the place to keep out unwanted guests."

"So how are we doing this, Boss Girl?" asked Bloodborne, turning to the team leader. "Slow and careful, or hard and fast?"

"Don't have time for slow and careful," she answered. She was grimacing with nausea, and the fiery glow in her belly was steadily growing brighter and brighter. "I'm going to power puke soon. We've got to get out of here before that happens. All this light pollution will mask my flames, stand back boys."

The two men hastily got out of the way as Neomi took a deep breath, and she doubled over vomiting a powerful stream of fire that burned a wide hole through the guarding fence and surged across the compound to smash through the side wall of the building. As soon as she managed to choke down the forceful stream and swallow it, all three of them hurried through the breach and into the plant.

The interior of the large building looked to be a dangerous place. Banks of machinery were on all sides, violet lightning surging between them at unpredictable intervals, and a sturdy wall of steel blocked entry to the heart of the plant. A single monstrous blast of flames from the small girl's mouth disintegrated the obstructing machinery and much of the wall before them, and their path was made clear. Alarm klaxons were blaring now and the lightning streams between the remaining machines had grown blazing-bright and frenzied, but nothing else impeded them as they entered the power core.

The core of the power plant was a spherical room overgrown with cables and screens and mysterious machinery, with catwalks leading over the central pit to the nucleus. Ominous radiation symbols and electrical hazard signs were on almost every surface. At the very centre of it all was a tall metal pillar with a circular catwalk ring around it for access. Square receptacles were slotted around the middle of the pillar, all of them dark and empty except for one, which was occupied by a violet-glowing metal cube the size of a cinder block. This, then, was the goal of their perilous quest.

"Hard to believe such a little thing could be the lifeblood of this entire blooming place," Bloodborne commented as they approached the pillar. "It's got to be worth a fortune. How the hell did the Legion get it?"

"Let's just figure out how *we're* going to get it," said Mindbreak, scrutinizing the cube. The glowing microfusion cell was securely held in place behind a panel of thick plexiglass, besides which was a keypad and a card reader slot. "We can't bypass the security on this thing. We'll have to brute-force it, but how?"

"I could smash that panel," said Bloodborne. "But I'll bet that would damage the cell. Boss Girl, think you can weld it open?"

"I'll try," Volcano Girl answered nervously. She opened her mouth and carefully let out a thin stream of flame, narrowing her lips to a small 'O' shape to focus her expulsion into an intense fire-jet only a foot or so in length. Bending over the console, she applied her flame jet to the side of the square plexiglass panel, quickly melting through the crease. One side after another, she traced the perimeter of the panel. Soon all four edges were melted molten furrows, glowing and steaming, and she swallowed her flame jet and sighed happily.

"Nice job. I know who to go to if I ever need to rob a bank," said Bloodborne with a grin. He reached for the panel, but Neomi caught his hand and stopped him.

"Let me. The heat won't affect me," she said. Ben nodded and stepped back. She proceeded to insert her fingers into the melted creases of the panel, digging through the soft molten plexiglass like putty. Straining and gasping, she slowly pulled the panel out of its housing, long strings of glowing melted glass trailing from the edges. Finally she managed to pull the obstacle out completely, and with a smile of triumph, she discarded the square of plexiglass and reached for the carry-handles protruding from the top of the cube. The power cell detached easily and slid out of its receptacle…

And then disaster struck. Violet lightning arced from the open receptacle to the bottom of the cube. Neomi froze in place, shaking violently as the massive electrical surge coursed through her small body. All the lights and instrumentation surrounding the trio started to flicker and dim as the full power of the plant drained from the core, and the fiery glow of the girl's belly swiftly changed to the same sizzling violet hue of the lightning that suffused her.

"*NEOMI!*" Ben screamed. He tried to snatch the cube away from her, but electricity shot into his hands before he even made contact, and he fell convulsing to the catwalk floor. Thinking fast, Mordecai quickly located a red lever marked "Emergency Shutdown" and yanked it down, but the catastrophe could not be undone.

Neomi was paralyzed, her head thrown back and every muscle in her body taut and twitching as all the power of the central core and fusion cell was vented into her fragile form. Her incensed stomach shot blazing heat up her throat and out her open mouth, but instead of fire, a mighty blast of crackling violet lightning exploded from her mouth straight upward into the shielding material of the core's ceiling. Panels, junctions, cables and valves all started to spark and shatter as the regurgitated electricity was reabsorbed by the dying power plant, and Mordecai flinched and raised his arms to cover his face as he was pelted with burning sparks.

The young girl was immobilized and helpless for a long time, uncontrollably vomiting the violet lightning into the ceiling of the core. Mordecai huddled over Ben's motionless form, spreading his open trench coat over them both to protect against the showers of sparks from above. By now the overloaded power plant was still and dark outside the core; the electricity arcing into Neomi's body from the pillar receptacle had long since ceased. Yet the lightning blasts kept shooting out of her, again and again and again, and Mord could only watch on helplessly as her stomach ejected the endless lightning out through her mouth in a brilliant show of self-sustaining power.

Several long minutes passed, yet slowly but surely, the conical lightning bursts spraying from the Volcano Girl's mouth were lessening in violence and intensity as her stomach gradually ceased to expel the flow of power. The microfusion cell in her hands was dark and depleted, but now its brilliant glow was emanating from within the girl's belly, its light undimmed even as the lightning coming out of her died away. Emergency lights came on, illuminating the now pitch-dark room in a dull, hellish red glare. The cube fell from her hands as her body relaxed, and Mord quickly moved to catch her as her wobbling legs gave out and she fell backward into his arms. Clouds of thick white smoke billowed from her mouth as she gasped and panted for breath, but she soon came out of her swoon and got her legs underneath her again.

"Neomi? Are you okay?" Mordecai gently asked as she stood up.

"I-I'm-*uuhh*!!"

Neomi tried to answer him, but lightning exploded from her mouth as soon as she opened it, and she doubled over retching as blazing electricity started spraying out of her again. The storm was as powerful and prolonged as before; Ben soon regained his senses and moved to Neomi's side to rub her heaving back as she threw up blast after blast of streaming violet lightning into the battered metal surfaces of the core walls. It was becoming obvious that her stomach was now generating this power on its own, and it was impossible for the superheroine to get it out of her. After another few minutes she eventually managed to stop vomiting the lightning, and she straightened up again and let out a soft sigh.

"Looks like the Volcano Girl just expanded her arsenal," Bloodborne commented wryly as she cautiously rubbed her violet-glowing belly. "How come when we get zapped you get a brand new superpower and all I get is tased?"

"Because her powers deal with energy and yours deal with blood," Mindbreak answered him in a casual manner-of-fact fashion. "I'm sure if we're infected with haemhorragic fever we'll get all the grief and you'll get all the gravy. Are you all right now Neomi?"

The Volcano Girl didn't answer. She clutched her glowing belly and clenched her teeth, struggling to resist her unrelenting nausea, but despite her best efforts her churning stomach abruptly forced a tingling, crackling surge up her throat, and lightning exploded from her mouth again as she doubled over retching forcefully. Every convulsive retch sent a shimmering globe of ball lightning flying from her mouth to burst in a massive detonation against the opposite wall, violet strokes of blazing electricity radiating in all directions from each point of impact like the tines of a sea urchin. She projectile-vomited several dozens of these lightning balls, one after another, utterly devastating the far wall of the core. Then she finally seemed to regain control of herself and slowly stood up straight.

"Feeling better now?" asked Bloodborne, gently patting her back. She rubbed her glowing belly and sighed, sending thick ribbons of white smoke billowing from her mouth.

"No," she said sourly. "I feel awful. My body is trying to adapt to this new power inside me, but it's so strong I can barely hold it in. My stomach is tingling so hard it feels like it's going to-*uuhh*!!"

The girl abruptly doubled over gushing lightning from her mouth again, but this time it was a single continuous beam rather than a ball or a conical blast, shooting straight across the room to carve a glowing furrow along the far wall. She seemed to have much better control of it this time; she straightened up and experimentally turned her head one way and the next as she aimed her mouth at the wall, tracing glowing molten lines over the surface like a laser cutting ray. The lightning stream kept coming out of her for several more minutes, straining even her well-trained breath control, but it did eventually cease, and she relaxed and drew several deep breaths.

"Well look at that!" said Ben in surprised admiration. Neomi had used her newly discovered lightning beam to carve a huge glowing 'V' shape into the spherical wall of the core. "V for Volcano Girl! That's badass, Boss!"

"Not bad," Mindbreak acknowledged coolly. "Now if you're finished playing with your new powers, we need to get going. The two Legionnaires upstairs are dead, but the others are starting to surround this facility. They're freaked out, but they'll be coming in here soon enough. Are you well enough to move?"

"As well as I'm going to be," the team leader said with a grimace, as the violet glow in her belly returned to its normal fiery hue. "God, I still feel horrible. I'm gonna power-puke again soon, but I think I can hold it in a little while longer. Let's get to that train in the back. Ben, grab that fusion cell, it might still come in handy."

"No can do," Bloodborne reported after a moment. He was squatting before the fallen cube, and he gave a tug on the handles to demonstrate the problem. The darkened cell was partially melted, its sagging underside fused to the metal catwalk.

"How about that. A fused fusion cell," Ben wisecracked. Neomi stifled a giggle, and Mord rolled his eyes. "Looks like junk now, Boss Girl. Still want me to bring it along?"

"No. I was hoping to charge it up with my lightning and use it to power the train maybe, but that's not going to work now," the girl explained. "We'll have to find some other way."

"We'll figure out something. But we've got to go. Now." said Mord urgently. " The Legionnaires are bringing something special for us. I hear it in their thoughts. Something special... for you, Neomi. They have some kind of new weapon... and they think they can finally defeat you with it. They call it 'the Tin Men'. And it's almost here."

"Oh s&@t! Let's get out of here!" Ben exclaimed. He started back toward the way they came from, but Mord caught his arm.

"That's where they're coming from. They want to trap us in here. We better go out the back door," said the sinister superhero.

In reply, Ben pointed to the rear entrance of the power core room, at the far wall. That entire half of the spherical core was a smoking half-melted ruin, the containment door itself barely visible within the warped slag of its frame.

"Can't get out that way dude!"

"Oh yes we can," the Volcano Girl countered in her soft unassuming voice, and she took a deep, deep breath.

"No wait Neomi! That's the turbine room!" Mindbreak yelled, but his voice was drowned out by the roar of the flames. A colossal blast of fire from the small girl's mouth disintegrated through the two-foot thick shielding wall and all the layers of machinery on both sides in a matter of seconds, surging into the vast adjoining room and nearly filling it up with utter conflagration. Neomi was extremely nauseous and couldn't stop vomiting forth the inferno for a long precious minute, but with a supreme effort she finally forced down the erupting flames and swallowed them, and she looked up to survey her handiwork as she panted for breath.

The rectangular turbine room was several stories deep and several more high, illuminated by the hellish red emergency backup lights in the ceiling, with two rows of giant turbine towers down the middle and a network of bridging catwalks and stairwells to access them. Everything was half melted to slag now, with few catwalks remaining between the listing, sagging turbines. The three young superhumans stared at the chasm before them in dismay.

"Oops," whispered Neomi in chagrin. "I think I overdid it a little."

"That's okay. That's okay," said Ben in forced nonchalance. "We can get through this. There are plenty of stairs left, we can climb down to the bottom and back up the other side…"

"No time! They're almost at the building!" Mord interrupted urgently.

"…or we can have our Girl barf up some some ice bridges…" the younger man continued.

"She's too sick for precision work now! She won't be able to control it!"

"… or we can do a tightrope act over the remaining bridges." he finished.

"Are you kidding me??" Mord almost shouted. "Do you see what's left of the catwalks?"
"You got any better ideas, bub?" Ben growled.

"Sure. Let's blow through another wall in the core," said the dark-clad superhuman.

"No, the core is in the centre of the plant. We'll just end up going deeper into the complex," Neomi spoke up. "The back wall has got to be at the end of this room. We'll go across the catwalks, it's our only chance. Ben, you carry me just like you did in the tunnel. I'll reinforce the supports with ice, I can still control myself enough for that. Mord, stay close. Let's go."

With a nod of acknowledgement, Bloodborne gently lifted his petite team leader into his arms and moved to the largest central catwalk. Volcano Girl retched several short bursts of freezing Cryoflame at the support struts at either side and below, coating the heat-warped structures with diamond-hard ice. With that, the lad gingerly stepped onto the heat-warped bridge and began making his way across, with Mindbreak right behind.

The damaged catwalk bridge creaked and swayed alarmingly as the heroes traversed it, with predictable effect on the Volcano Girl. Fire burst from her mouth every few paces, great roiling jets of it, but she managed to keep partial control of it and aimed the fireblasts safely upward without slipping into uncontrolled vomiting. It was a slow, harrowing journey. Bloodborne tried to ignore the fire gushing from the girl's mouth just beside his head, Volcano Girl did her best to control her somersaulting stomach as the catwalk bucked and undulated beneath them, and Mindbreak struggled to keep his balance and not think of the looming chasm below and all around them. The catwalks mercifully did not collapse, and the trio were soon just a dozen yards or so from the rear wall of the turbine room.

"Oh hell. Incoming on our six!" Mindbreak suddenly warned.

Bloodborne and the Volcano Girl looked back behind them toward the core. Legionnaires had entered the cavernous turbine room. Only a half dozen were on the landing proper, but many more of the altered gangers were behind them, their eyes and veins glowing an eerie blue in the near-dark. And all of them were armed with guns.

Raging flames instantly exploded from Neomi's mouth. Mord dropped to one knee to dodge the flames as the thundering blast shot over Ben's shoulder toward the far landing, burning through the platform and much of the bridge in seconds. On this end the ice-bolstered bridge struts held, though the catwalk sagged alarmingly down toward the centre precipice. The six Legionnaires hastily retreated back to the core as the flames washed over the landing, and they took cover behind the shelter of the core walls.

The Volcano Girl finished her mighty expulsion and drew a deep breath, and she started retching forcefully at their distant foes, blazing fireballs flying from her mouth with every retch to detonate amongst the hiding gangers like incendiary grenades. However, after a moment Mindbreak held up a hand.

"Wait, Neomi. They're not attacking."

The girl tried to stop, but her stomach wouldn't stop churning, and she projectile-vomited several more fireballs across the room before she managed to swallow the erupting fire and cease her assault. An eerie silence descended as the mortal enemies stared at each other, Legionnaires and superheroes, from opposite sides of the chasm.

"Why aren't they shooting? Maybe they wouldn't hit us through Boss Girl's flames, but since when did that ever stop 'em?" Bloodborne growled.

"They don't want to hurt us. Well, they don't care about you and me, but they won't risk hitting Neomi. They want her alive."

"Nice to be loved," said Bloodborne sarcastically. "They must really think those Tin Men got a shot. Let's not give them a chance to find out, huh?"

With a nod, the Volcano Girl turned her head forward to look at the end of the turbine room. On this side there was a long screen of thick plexiglass through which a large control room of sorts was visible, with banks of monitors and instruments before rows of chairs. There was a pair of large bulkhead doors leading into this control room, but there were keypads and card readers beside them and they were likely locked. Taking a deep breath, she vomited a monstrous blast of fire at the rear wall, burning through plexiglass and steel and plastic alike to surge into the control room and through its back wall as well. When she finished expelling the flames, a glowing tunnel was revealed, boring straight through the power plant's structure and out into the back yard. The superheroine took another breath and retched another blast through the tunnel, this time of wintry Cryoflame, and when that was done the tunnel was cooled and traversable.

The team made their way down the remainder of the catwalk, and Bloodborne set his team leader on her feet before moving quickly through the tunnel, watching and listening for trouble. Mindbreak was right behind him, and after an apprehensive glance back at the distant unmoving Legionnaires still within the plant, Volcano Girl followed.

Ben stopped short of the opening leading to the outside.

"Trouble," he reported. "I hear a lot of hydraulics out there, mechanical moving parts. Construction machines maybe. Multiple sources, and close. Mord, what are you getting?"

Mindbreak frowned. "Uh… what the? … Nothing. I can't sense anybody out there. Must be drones or robots."

"Tin Men. It fits," said Volcano Girl. "Okay guys, get behind me. I'm not gonna hold back, so hopefully this will be quick."

Neomi gingerly approached the melted aperture and poked her head out. What she saw made her wince with fear, and she pulled back and steeled herself. It was game time.

Large metallic figures were waiting for them outside, arrayed in a semi-circle just within the outer fence to surround the back wall of the building. They were humanoid-shaped but over eight feet tall, the central blocky torso extruding segmented arms with large hydraulic pincers and sturdy reinforced legs with wide-padded feet. Blue-glowing eyes gazed out from a tiny plexiglass slit within each heavy helmet. Flat surfaces were painted bright red, with a prominent hazard symbol on the chestplate, and every joint and moving part was shielded with a thick layer of corrugated black plastic. *Exosuits.* The final weapon of the Legion was revealed, and the only way to reach the distant train engine was through them.

True to her word, the Volcano Girl did not hold back. Stepping forward, Neomi shot out a tremendous blast of fire from her mouth, sweeping the stream back and forth to completely immolate the group of armoured Legionnaires. The giant figures staggered back within the inferno, shoved off balance by the sheer force of the flames, but... did not disintegrate. When the roiling clouds of fire dissipated, the exosuits were revealed almost unmarred, just dusted with a little ash and smoking slightly. Astonished, she spewed out an even more powerful blast at them, but they were ready for it and braced themselves, and when the conflagration faded they were unharmed as before. The Volcano Girl's flames were ineffective.

Only the mighty enforcer of the Legion, Nemesis himself, had ever emerged from Neomi's fire unscathed. For a whole team of Legionnaires to withstand it, not just surviving but left fully functional, spelled disaster for the young superheroine and her allies.

As one, the exosuits advanced on her position, leaning forward to brace against her repeated expulsions of fire. They were slow and plodding, but inexorable. Neomi rapidly cycled through her various fire-vomit powers; the armoured suits were unharmed even by the immense solar power of her Sunflare blasts, impeded only a moment by her gluey lava-like Magmite, and completely unscathed by her corrosive Plasma. In desperation she changed her attacks to Cryoflame, attempting to freeze the lumbering goliaths solid, but even the coatings of super-hard ice held them back only a moment before they shattered through the impediment and continued on.

"Fall back!" she gasped, retreating to where her companions still stood, within the outer wall of the power plant. "I can't hurt these things! We have to find another way out!"

"There's no time! They're right outside the hole!" said Bloodborne urgently, as the heavy footsteps drew closer. "Mord, mess with their heads and slow them up! Hurry!"

"I can't!" exclaimed Mindbreak. "I can't feel their minds at all. Those suits must be lead-lined, I can't reach the pilots!"

"Okay then, try your lightning! That might work on them!" Bloodborne said to Volcano Girl. She shook her head, gazing wide-eyed at him.

"Ben, it's too soon! The lightning is too strong for me to control right now, I'll power-puke all over the whole cavern if I try to use it!" she explained.

"Go ahead and do it then! Let it all out!" Bloodborne urged her, even as the first of the exosuits came into view. "We're out of options! Do it!"

The girl took a deep, deep breath, and the fiery glow of her belly rapidly changed to a sizzling violet hue. Great metal pincers reached out for her, ready to claim her as the prize prisoner of the Legion. The Legion's victory was literally within their grasp. And then, the Volcano Girl unleashed the full might of her terrible power upon them.

Hunching forward, Neomi explosively vomited forth a great torrent of violet lightning, the blazing, crackling blast enveloping the lead exosuit and washing over it to surge into the cavern beyond. The Legion machine staggered back within the torrent, sparking and twitching and stalling, and within seconds it went still and limp, still standing but with arms dangling loosely like a puppet with its strings cut. Outside, half of the vast cavern was filled with lightning from the giant wide-angled cone spraying from the girl's mouth, a titanic maelstrom of blinding-bright electrical arcs striking at every object and surface in the main trainyard. Active machines and vehicles stalled and sparked and smoked, unsheltered Legionnaires collapsed and convulsed and quickly went still and silent. None of the exosuits were spared, all suffering the same fate as the lead machine. And still the storm persisted.

The Volcano Girl had fallen to her knees, gripping her bright-glowing belly and retching convulsively as the lightning spouted from her mouth, on and on and on. Every now and then the storm began to wane as she struggled to stop, only to explode out of her at full strength seconds later. Bloodborne squatted beside her and comfortingly rubbed her heaving back as she threw up blast after prolonged blast into the cavern; her volatile new power had fearsomely incited her stomach, which was now intent on venting out more lightning than she could possibly control. She was vomiting so hard that she could barely breathe, her agonizing nausea so intense that tears of pain were leaking down her face. It felt like it had when her cancer had just manifested, every hourly power-puking fit so violent that she wanted to die to make it stop.

But Neomi wasn't a helpless little girl anymore. She was a veteran superhero now, with many victories and enemy kills to her name, and she was no longer at the mercy of her illness. Drawing on the deepest reserves of her inner strength, she began to calm herself despite the ferocious convulsions of vomiting wracking her fragile body, and mercifully the overwhelming nausea began to subside. It took another minute of struggling with her erupting stomach, but she finally managed to choke down the stream of lightning and swallow it. Her belly bulged taut and tingling with the strain of containing her immense new power, but the Volcano Girl was the master of her body once again.

Bloodborne helped her to her feet as his team leader stood up and surveyed her handiwork. The cavern would be completely dark, with all the lights and vehicles gone inert, but flammable materials here and there had caught fire and were giving some illumination to the trainyard. Almost everything was scorched and smoking: debris, bodies, structures and machines, including the exosuits. Her new Electroflame power had handily removed all opposition before them.

Glowing eyes were peering out from within the visor slits of the exosuit helmets, directing wrathful glares and muffled cursing at the team. The operators were evidently still alive, their environmental protection suits having absorbed the massive electrical charge from the Volcano Girl's eruption, but the suits themselves appeared to be burnt out and inoperative. Some of the exosuits were slightly rocking back and forth as the trapped Legionnaires struggled to escape; one of the suits actually fell over, knocking down two other nearby suits like dominoes, and the swearing from within grew even louder and angrier.

"Look at that. We've gone from Tin Men to Tinned Men," Ben deadpanned. He went up to one of the exosuits and knocked on the chestplate, and watched on as the machine slowly toppled over. He made an exaggerated shrug. "Guess you boys could really use a can opener about now, huh?"

Mordecai wasn't terribly amused by Ben's clowning, but Neomi couldn't help but squeak with laughter, and she immediately retched out a heavy shower of crackling sparks. Mord looked at her with some concern and said: "How are you feeling Neomi?"

"A little better," she answered. "That storm-puke took a lot of pressure off my stomach. I'm ready to move when you are."

"Well let's move right now," said the dark-clad superhuman, looking back at the undamaged half of the cavern where distant angry shouts were becoming audible. "You've bought us some time, but we're going to have a lot of company real soon."

The team moved out, heading for the train engine not far from the plant. As they drew close, Ben winced as they saw the smoking scorch marks along the body of the engine car. "Uh-oh. I think you fried it, Boss. We might have to get out of here on foot."

"Maybe not," said Mord thoughtfully. He drew closer and peered within the control cabin. "The controls look intact. This machine wasn't running when it got hit, it might still be functional."

"Let's get in and give it a shot," ordered the team leader. "It'll get us out of sight at least. Ben, give me a hand."

Once inside, Mindbreak moved swiftly to the control console and examined it. He was the only one who had any technical proficiency at all, and after a moment spent examining the controls and readouts, he flipped a switch and turned a dial, and gave a rare smile as the panel lit up.

"Bingo. It still works," he reported. "The main battery looks like it's dead though, we've only got emergency power. That won't take us far."

"That's fine. We've got another battery ready to go," Ben grinned, and he playfully poked Neomi's swollen belly, which was still glowing a coruscating violet light from within. Even this gentle touch made Neomi retch out another shower of sparks, and she glared at him, though only half-seriously.

"Ben's right. We have all the power we need," she said, looking down at her belly. "We just have to figure out how to get it out of me and into the train's system."

"Give me a second," said Mordecai, his eye falling on several large panels on the wall around the control console. The centremost panel slid open at his touch, revealing a compartment filled with tightly fitted machinery, at the center of which was a metal cube in a receptacle almost identical to that which they had seen in the power plant's core. A prominent label above the receptacle read: 'PRIMARY POWER CELL'.

"Here we are," said Mord, nonchalantly pointing at the battery cell. "Neomi, I believe you know what to do. Gently though, give it only what it can absorb."

Neomi nodded eagerly and moved into position before the open panel. Bending over it, she carefully vomited lightning into the receptacle, disgorging a stream of violet electricity that surrounded and suffused the cube. Nothing happened at first, but as she continued expelling the stream into the receptacle, the cube began to faintly glow the same violet colour. Diode lights came on within the engine compartment, and then the strip lamps overhead lit up and illuminated the cabin. Mord slammed his hand down on a large green button on the control console, and with a growling hum the train's engine turned over and powered up. He grabbed the throttle lever.

"And we're off!" Ben crowed triumphantly as the train car lurched into motion. "Fasten your seatbelts ladies and gentlemen, next stop Anywhere-But-Here Station! Yeehaw!"

Grimacing with motion sickness, Neomi forced herself to stop spewing the lightning into the engine compartment and looked up, right as the closed gate of the power plant yard came into view.

"Hang on!" cried Mordecai, and he punched the throttle to full power. The train car surged forward, and the cabin shook as they crashed through the swing gate in an instant. Ben grabbed Neomi about the shoulders and braced her against his body as he grabbed a guard rail with his other hand. But despite his swift reaction, the sudden motion was too much for the girl's stomach and lightning exploded from her mouth again, smashing through the front windscreen and spraying across the trainyard in a wide sweeping cone.

"Ah crap. Every bastard in this place saw that," snarled Mindbreak. As the Volcano Girl struggled to stop erupting, he cast an eye back behind them, and winced. "Guys, we've got a lot of company coming!"

Behind them, a horde of Legionnaires were chasing after the train car, steadily gaining on them with their unnatural sprinting speed. Their eyes blazed with rage, bared fangs gleaming in the near dark, whooping and howling as they closed on their prey. Thinking fast, Bloodborne lifted the featherlight superheroine off the ground from behind and swung her around, even as the stream of lightning continued spraying from her mouth. The blazing stream smashed through the cabin's side windows and then the back windows as Ben turned Neomi to face the rear of the train, toward the crowd of pursuing Legionnaires.

The Volcano Girl's lightning cone swept through the crowd; some jumped high or dived to the side and escaped, but most of the altered gangers collapsed to the ground twitching and smoking as they ceased their pursuit. Yet the more of them she cut down, even more heedlessly joined the chase, and she struggled to keep control of herself as she threw up blast after crackling blast into the howling horde at their heels.

Then, there was a thudding impact on the ceiling of the control cabin. And then, another.

"Seriously? They're hanging off the roof now?!" Bloodborne snarled, whipping his gaze from side to side as glaring blue-glowing eyes appeared at both side windows.

"Hold them off! We're almost out!" Mindbreak snapped, without lifting his gaze from the touchscreen map displaying the rail track network. Unbeknownst to his companions, he had been frantically aligning the oncoming track junctions to set a path that would take them to one of the intact exit tunnels, and he had come within seconds of derailing the car several times. He didn't dare to take his attention off what he was doing for even an instant.

Everything was happening in a blur of motion, of action and reaction and counteraction. The Legionnaire at the smashed side window was thrusting his hand into the cabin, bringing a vicious-looking submachinegun to bear. The one at the other side window drove his fist into the glass, bashing through the obstacle and showering Mindbreak with flying shards. With superhuman speed and strength of his own, Bloodborne whipped his tentacles around the arm of the gun-wielding thug and yanked him inside, throwing the metahuman's whole body across the cabin and out the other side window to collide with his compatriot. The Legionnaires disappeared into the darkness, cursing and flailing as they fell from the train car, and the lad let out a bark of triumph.

"No ticket no ride, chumps!"

As if in grim reply, there were several additional thuds of booted feet landing on the ceiling of the cabin. Both of the young men cast annoyed glances upward.

"You better go tell them," Mindbreak advised, brushing shattered glass from his hat and clothing. Bloodborne bared his teeth as he scrambled out the side window to meet the hijackers.

"VIP Section only! Get your asses back to Economy!" Ben hollered as he pulled himself up to the roof. Three Legionnaires were up topside, finding their feet on the speeding train, and the lad promptly threw himself right into their midst, blood-appendages whipping and slicing all about him.

All three young superheroes were quickly embroiled in their individual struggles. Mindbreak fought to keep their train car upright and headed the right way, Bloodborne wrestled with the hostile boarders on the train's roof, and the Volcano Girl held back the might of the entire Legion contingent chasing them from the rear.

The battle was not going well, for any of the three. Time and again, Mindbreak was forced to slow down when the train rounded a bend or ploughed through some debris on the track. That gave opportunity for more Legionnaires to leap onto the train and engage with Bloodborne. The lad was just as fast and strong as his foes, and he could regenerate his injuries and produce weapons of blood to aid him, but he couldn't hold his own against so many of the bestial gangers at once. And Volcano Girl had been vomiting violently and continuously for some time now and was at the brink of exhaustion, while the Legion chasing them seemed indefatigable. The heroes were fighting a battle of attrition, and they were losing.

Salvation came suddenly.

"*Ben, get down!*" Mindbreak's ghost-voice urgently whispered into Bloodborne's ear.

Sensing what was coming, the lad dropped down flat amidst his assailants, suffering some nasty machete-gashes in the process. Suddenly the darkness of a tunnel engulfed them, and those Legionnaire hijackers that didn't jump off in time were knocked away by the lip of the tunnel roof.

Realizing what was happening, Volcano Girl ceased spewing forth her lightning stream, took a deep, deep breath, and unleashed the full might of her terrible power. A titanic inferno-blast of flames erupted from her small mouth to surge through the tunnel behind them, deluging the entire trainyard cavern with fire before the roof began to cave in. Little in the trainyard was spared immolation save perhaps the trapped exosuit pilots, though whether they could dig themselves out after the cavern collapsed was another matter entirely.

"PUNCH IT BISHOP!!" Ben yowled down from the train car roof, hoping that Mord would at least hear him telepathically through the raging din of the flames and falling rocks. He cast an eye back at the conflagration behind them, rapidly gaining on them as the collapsing tunnel constricted all the space and air available to the flames. The backwash of heat flooded over him, and the rear of the train began to sag and melt. Disaster seemed imminent…

And then the train car zoomed out from a topside subway tunnel, exploding forth in a great fountain of fire like a boulder ejected from an active volcano. The Volcano Girl herself threw her head back and allowed the almighty flame geyser blasting forth from her mouth to shoot straight up into the sky, lighting up the core of Meridian City like the dawning of a second sun, much like the eruption she had unleashed at the beginning of the night's adventure. Bloodborne whooped and cheered in triumph, and with a sigh of relief Mindbreak eased down the throttle and took off his hat to wipe his brow. The velocity of the speeding train slowly dwindled, as did the volume of the flames shooting out of the Volcano Girl, and both eventually ceased entirely.

Neomi sagged tiredly against the half-melted back wall of the train cabin, blowing out thick clouds of billowing white smoke as she panted for breath, and Ben came over and kindly offered his shoulder, which she gratefully took and allowed herself to be led to the conductor's chair. Mord looked back through the shattered, melted aperture and thoughtfully scrutinized the burning rubble that was all that remained of the subway tunnel they just exited.

"Is that it? We won? We're safe now?" he queried his team.

"Hell yeah!" Ben exclaimed. "Boss Girl brought the roof down on the whole cave. There's no way anybody's gonna dig their way out of that any time soon."

"Looks like we won," Neomi agreed, still panting for breath. "Even if they could recover some assets from the site, the operation itself is finished. There won't be any mass transit for the Legion now."

"And their Tin Men got canned to boot," said Ben happily. "Even if we ever see 'em again, Neomi's got a brand new barf-blast to deal with them. We got in there, ninja'd their power supply, leveled-up the Boss, and crashed the place on the way out. Sounds like a big win for Team Volcano to me!"

There was a long pause as Ben's words sunk in. Their fledgling team had destroyed a massive Legion operation all by themselves. This was a major victory, not just for the three young heroes but for all the superheroes and good citizens of Meridian. The Legion had just suffered a staggering loss of materiel and manpower, and the Volcano Girl was even more powerful as a result. Word of this would spread, villains would tremble, and colleagues and citizens would rejoice. Tonight, the good guys were triumphant.

"Well, fine. Score one for our side," Mindbreak spoke up, breaking the silence. "But if we're going to go on like this, we'll need a better name than 'Team Volcano'."

"What what what? Does that mean you want to stay on our team?" Bloodborne teased him. "Holy smoke, I do believe that someone's had a change of heart!"

"Yeah, yeah. Don't rub it in," Mord groused. Neomi couldn't help but squeak with laughter, and she retched fire twice through her giggles before she got her mirth and her stomach under control. Once she was settled, Mordecai went on: "We've got our problems, sure, but we work well together. I don't want to break up a good thing. Besides, you need me. You'd be chalk outlines if not for me, you know that."

"He's right," Neomi broke in quickly before Ben could retort. "There's no way we could have made it through that place without his powers and his know-how. We need him."

"What about your problems with the Boss' powers, then?" Ben asked, turning serious. "What happened to the 'unstable time bomb' and all that talk? Changed your mind?"

"Put simply, yes," Mord replied. "I've seen what she can do now, and I've felt in her mind how she turned her disadvantage to an advantage. That's some pretty tough mojo right there. It's still problematic, but I think we can make it work. And we've all seen what we can accomplish together."

Neomi exchanged a long glance with Ben. Then she reached out a hand, and grasped Mordecai's hand in warm acceptance.

"Welcome to the team," she said sincerely. Ben put his hand over theirs, making it a three-way handclasp, and then, just for a moment, the ghostly mist-hand of Zhen Xiaolong materialized over the clasp to make it a four-way, giving his blessing to the newborn super-team. It was done. After a moment Ben withdrew his hand and grinned impishly.

"All this team spirit is all well and good, but can we mosey on out of here now? Sun's coming up. It's a whole new day, and we got some major partying to do!"

The sun was indeed coming up. A new day was dawning, lighting up the horizon with rosy-hued light. Mordecai wordlessly pushed the throttle lever, and the battered train car leisurely picked up steam. This one train had survived the Legion base's destruction, and its path took them directly to the east, to the uptown district and reunion with colleagues, friends and family. Eastward it rode, on into the sunrise, and the hopes and aspirations of a new force for good rode with it.

FIN

ABOUT THE AUTHOR

Arvind V. Jagessar is a life long science fiction and fantasy fan who after reading dozens of novels finally decided to write his own. He also enjoys video games of the sci fi and fantasy flavour (naturally!) and role playing games, both excellent training for visualizing and writing fiction. Originally from the Caribbean, Arvind has lived in the northern Ontario city of Sudbury, Canada, and has no plans to change his location or entertainment preferences. He can be reached at:

arv_email@yahoo.com

mist-hand of Zhen Xiaolong materialized over the clasp to make it a four-way, giving his blessing to the newborn super-team. It was done. After a moment Ben withdrew his hand and grinned impishly.

"All this team spirit is all well and good, but can we mosey on out of here now? Sun's coming up. It's a whole new day, and we got some major partying to do!"

The sun was indeed coming up. A new day was dawning, lighting up the horizon with rosy-hued light. Mordecai wordlessly pushed the throttle lever, and the battered train car leisurely picked up steam. This one train had survived the Legion base's destruction, and its path took them directly to the east, to the uptown district and reunion with colleagues, friends and family. Eastward it rode, on into the sunrise, and the hopes and aspirations of a new force for good rode with it.

FIN

ABOUT THE AUTHOR

Arvind V. Jagessar is a life long science fiction and fantasy fan who after reading dozens of novels finally decided to write his own. He also enjoys video games of the sci fi and fantasy flavour (naturally!) and role playing games, both excellent training for visualizing and writing fiction. Originally from the Caribbean, Arvind has lived in the northern Ontario city of Sudbury, Canada, and has no plans to change his location or entertainment preferences. He can be reached at:

arv_email@yahoo.com

Made in the
USA
Middletown, DE